RICHARD GARCIA MORGAN

The Hidden Island

Tales from Mysterion, Book 1

WAYSTONE
PRESS

First published by Waystone Press, www.waystonepress.com in 2017

Copyright © Richard Garcia Morgan, 2018

First Edition

ISBN: 978-1-7750695-0-8

This book was professionally typeset on Reedsy.
Find out more at reedsy.com

Get a Free Gift!

Building a relationship with my readers is one of the best parts of the writing life. I send out occasional newsletters to my Readers' Group with interesting curated content, as well as details of new releases in the Tales of Mysterion and special offers.

And if you sign up to my Readers' Group, I'll send you an audio excerpt from Book 2, *The Falls of Mysterion,* FOR FREE.

You can find the link to sign up for my Readers' Group at the end of this novel.

To my mother, Myrith

I

Part One

1

Chapter One

A bluebottle fly skimmed over an empty ocean. He had been travelling for several days, and now his destination rose above the horizon: an immense bonfire seeming to float on the surface of the water.

Reaching the edge of the flames, the fly pushed through without being singed. Beyond, a storm assaulted him, winds tossing him around, threatening to hurl him into the black waters, until a random gust threw him forward. Now waves were breaking in an uproar of foam. An island loomed out of the darkness, and the bluebottle tumbled toward the beach.

Beyond the breakers, the air calmed to the consistency of warm mud. Ahead, the bluebottle spied the sentries slumped unconscious under the twisted mangroves at the beachhead. He considered transforming early but decided against it. They might wake, there would be questions, and he would account for every wasted minute. So he spun above their heads, penetrating the thickest part of the mangrove forest before unfolding into the natural form of the Djinn—a human body with the wings of a Pterodactyl and a skeletal head with spreading horns.

After dodging through the trees, he broke out into a clearing of black sand. At the center of the clearing glittered a pool, and beside it rose a great, bloated baobab tree whose branches clawed up at the clouds and the full moon. Lord Geist waited in the tree's shadow, hunched in his cloak.

The Djinn landed and bowed before Lord Geist, pressing his horns into the sand.

"My Lord," he began. "Great and high and exalted—"

"You are late! Were you seen?"

"Of course not! I got close too, right in the tree above the Eld—uh, that is—above the *tyrant's* place of council..."

"Perhaps he knew you were there. Perhaps he fed you some stories. After all, Malach," Lord Geist's voice softened, "you have never been very good at imitating bluebottle flies."

I do it better than you, Malach thought.

"Oh really!" Lord Geist snapped. "And I suppose you think you are better in other ways, too?"

Malach cursed himself for not concealing his thoughts in Lord Geist's presence.

"I am not the fool you think I am, Malach," Lord Geist said. "I will answer your insolence yet. Now, report!"

Malach repeated word for word what he had overheard and committed to memory many days before.

"You are sure he said that?" Lord Geist demanded.

"Yes, Lord."

"That this boy would defeat me."

"Yes, Lord."

"Me."

"Yes."

Lord Geist shuffled to the edge of the pool and gazed at his dim reflection. Behind him, Malach dragged himself forward. At once Lord Geist turned, clutching his cloak about him.

"Not too close!"

Malach shrank away, but as soon Lord Geist's back was turned, Malach slithered forward again, craning his neck to see around him. Dangling from Lord Geist's hand was a chain attached to what looked like a lump of coal. Malach stared as Lord Geist lowered the pendant into the water and swirled it three times before withdrawing it into his cloak. As the ripples settled, the two Djinn's reflections dissolved into another image—a boy, his eyes closed, floating on a sea so clear that his shadow could be seen on the white sandy bottom. The boy was short and wiry, with coffee skin and the face of a cherub. Then the boy opened his eyes and stood, the water lapping his shoulders. As he looked into the distance, his jaw tightened, revealing stubborn lines beneath his rounded features.

Hard to pin this one down, Malach thought.

Lord Geist spun around.

"I thought I told you to stay back!"

"I wanted to see him," the younger Djinn whined.

"*I* want you to do as you are told!"

"He's not what I expected," Malach said, shuffling closer still.

"He is *exactly* what I expected," Lord Geist replied. "The old fool always prefers weakness over strength. Sending a child to defeat *me*!" He slapped at the pool, and the boy's image rippled and faded.

"What will you do?" Malach asked. "The boy can't do anything. He's not even fifteen! The Elder must be wrong..."

"Don't call him that!" Lord Geist shouted. "He is not your elder! I am your one true Elder. *He* is a tyrant!"

"Forgive me, lord." Malach bowed his head to the ground.

"As to *him* being wrong," Lord Geist continued. "We must be sure. We are so close to freedom..."

Silence fell as Lord Geist considered the matter. Finally, he glanced at Malach and inclined his head toward the Baobab tree. From somewhere in that direction came the sound of muffled screaming. Lord Geist smiled. "The tyrant uses the father to bring the son against me. That works both ways."

Malach scratched at his head with one long fingernail.

"And you want to be an Elder?" Lord Geist scoffed. "Think!"

Suddenly, Malach hopped up and down.

"I see!" he cried. "The father is our bait!"

"Yes," Lord Geist said patiently. "And then..."

"And when the father is used up, the son will be ours!"

"Exactly," Lord Geist said. "Do you think you are up to the task?"

"Me?" Malach said. "I am flattered that—"

"Don't be. I just don't trust you here by yourself anymore."

"I shall try to regain your trust by this, Lord." Malach bowed, trying to keep the glee out of his voice.

"You had better," Lord Geist replied. "Or your life will be forfeit." He shuffled to the tree. The screams were louder now. "You will appear to the boy in the form of his father." He grinned. "A good old-fashioned ghost at midnight."

"But..." Malach said, "how will I convince him? It won't make sense—"

"Use your imagination! Or would you rather I send someone else? Bagat, perhaps."

"No, Lord!" Malach cried. "I will accomplish it, I promise!"

"Good," Lord Geist said. Plunging his claws into the base of the tree trunk, he tore open a large gap, and the screams assaulted them, echoing through the interior. The Djinn stepped into the tree, closing it behind them. The air inside was a soup of old sweat and sewage, but the Djinn didn't seem to notice. Lord Geist raised one claw and chanted something in an unknown language. Immediately, a blue flame burst into life just above his palm.

In the dim, wavering light the interior of the Tree was a hollow space filled with a mound of tangled roots. As they descended several steps, the light reflected on something pale—the dirty face of a man, his body so enveloped in roots that it was no longer visible. The man's eyes were closed, turning side to side as he continued to shout incoherently, lost in a nightmare.

Lord Geist squatted down and shook the man awake. Haunted, unfocused eyes stared up at the Djinn.

"Who is it?" the prisoner shouted. "Elizabeth? Is that you?"

"No," Lord Geist whispered. "It is I, my dear Francis."

"I'm sorry, Liza," the man said. "I couldn't watch them take it all...!"

"Don't fret," Lord Geist whispered, raising his forefinger. "*I* have it all now. Just need a little more blood though..." With a quick motion, Lord Geist slashed at the man's cheek, ignoring his scream and allowing the black welling blood to coat his claw. Then he and Malach left the tree.

Outside, Malach waded knee-deep into the pool, and Lord Geist carefully anointed him with the blood. The Elder draped the pendant over the younger Djinn's neck, Malach quivering with excitement.

"Do not get too comfortable," Lord Geist warned. "You have no authority without my cloak. And that you will have to take from my dead body."

"I know," Malach replied. "May I say the words now?"

"Yes. And do not return without the boy. Return alone and your life belongs to me. Do you understand?"

"Yes, yes."

"Remember your place. You are not an Elder yet."

Malach did not reply. He lifted the pendant toward the spotlight of the moon and began to chant. His body glowed red, brightening until he cried out and dissolved among the reflections on the pool.

Lord Geist stared down at the ripples for a while before turning and shuffling to the tree. He leaned his horns close and nodded with satisfaction. The prisoner's screams had faded to moaning. Lord Geist stroked the pregnant trunk.

"Do not worry, my dear Francis," he whispered. "Your son is coming to join your dreams."

2

Chapter Two

Jonah Comfait floated in the shallows, his eyes following gold clouds across the sky. The equatorial water was exactly the temperature of his blood so that he felt the water only where it swirled around him on the surface, rising and subsiding with the waves, or when a current caressed his back. A monsoon breeze flowed over his stomach, face, and feet, but he could hear nothing underwater except the mute hiss of waves on the beach.

At last, he felt the air cool. He stood up. The wind had eased, but he could still hear the coconut fronds rattling along the beach behind him. Far ahead, the line of the reef had thickened, and Isle Decouvre seemed to be retreating as the end of the day approached. *Tide's turning*, Jonah thought

Sails appeared on the horizon. *A schooner!* Pain cut Jonah's chest, as he remembered the *Integrity* slipping easily among the anchored fishing *pirogues*, the seagoing dhows on their way to Arabia, and the luxury yachts registered in Nassau. She heeled in the morning breeze, her green-and-gold pennants fluttering. The letters on her hull advertised, "Mysterion Tours."

Then she was nudging the dock. The crew hauled down the few remaining sails with a crackling sound, while Jonah's father leaned over the rail and grinned at Jonah like a pirate with new-found treasure.

A more recent memory took its place—*Integrity*, her masts stripped even of their pennants, towed into the harbor by the Coast Guard. Jonah tried to push the scene away, but it was too late. The Coast Guard captain had bowed his balding head and fingered the brim of his cap as he spoke: *... found it grounded on one of the middle islands,* he had said. *The hull was abandoned, rigging a mess. The storm must have caught him, swept him overboard, and driven the ship ashore...*

The captain had spoken to Jonah's mother in Creole, to exclude him. Just because he went to the International School, they thought he couldn't understand. *I can tell what you're saying,* Jonah had snapped.

Jonah, that's rude, his mother had said.

Well, I can! He had shouted. *He needn't try to hide the truth from me.*

Jonah heard the snapping of branches. His mother had emerged from the trees at the head of the beach and was walking down to the water, stepping from one piece of driftwood to another to avoid thorns in the sand. Though her feet were bare, she wore the long-sleeved black dress she had put on for his father's memorial service. How straight she had sat in the pew that day, while women in flowery hats lit candles and wept theatrically, men wearing black armbands murmured among themselves, and the mingled odor of *Eau de Cologne*, incense, and sweaty bodies stifled his breathing. Jonah felt his throat closing at the memory.

As if she had heard his thoughts, his mother looked up and met his eyes. Her dark face had a muddy pallor, and her almond eyes were bruised with sleeplessness. She had not cried at the funeral, nor during the endless condolences afterwards, but every night since, her soft weeping from the other side of his bedroom wall had kept Jonah awake. She wore the black dress every day.

Why does she do that? he thought. *She shouldn't do that!* He tunneled his toes into the hard-packed sand until it changed from sugary fineness to the cool gravel of broken shells and coral. *I won't get out of the water,* he resolved. *She'll have to make me do it.*

His mother was now standing with the waves breaking over her bare brown feet. She seemed smaller from this distance—girlish and lonely against the white of the beach.

"Are you coming home?"

"In a bit," Jonah replied.

"Sunset and curfew is in half an hour."

"I know. I'll be in."

Jonah excavated a shell with his toes.

"I have something to tell you," she said. "Harry came by."

He did not reply. Harry Payet was a friend of the family. He had come back to the house after the memorial service and sat with Jonah's mother for a long time, holding her hand.

"I accepted his offer to buy the company," she said. "Debts and all."

Something gave way in Jonah's chest.

"Jonah, did you hear what I said?"

"I heard."

"We can pay off the mortgage and the bills now—"

"Dad would've paid them off."

"No, Jonah." Her voice was low. "It was past that point."

Jonah turned the shell in his fingers. Then he dropped it, watching it sway down through the clear water. When it touched bottom, he shoved it into the sand with his toe.

"Harry works for the government," he said.

His mother shook her head. "Everyone works for the government now."

"Fine." Jonah turned away to look at the reef. He felt dry inside.

"Do you want us to be out on the street?" she demanded.

He did not reply.

"The bank was going to foreclose. The business was bankrupt!"

"I know that!" Jonah said, raising his voice.

"So what did you expect me to do?" his mother cried. "Your father wouldn't sell out. He kept on saying how he would fix everything. But it just got worse. And now it's too late, and I have to pull us out of this hole we're in! What did you expect me to do when someone comes along who can help?"

"I don't know!" His voice shook as he fought his tears.

"Well, I had to make some decision. Otherwise, we are going to—"

Jonah ducked beneath the surface and pulled himself as far out toward the reef as he could. Only when his lungs started to hurt did he surface. The water had barely deepened—he could still touch the sand with his feet, and the reef seemed no closer. The sun had dropped behind the island. Isle Decouvre was now barely a smudge floating on the horizon.

The small figure of his mother was striding back toward the house. From the way she was walking, quickly and with her head bowed, he could tell that she was crying, ignoring the thorns under the sand.

Perhaps Dad really is gone—and for the first time, Jonah did not deny it.

Tears prickled his eyes. He wanted to break for the beach as fast as he could. Perhaps he could catch up to her before she reached the house. He could say sorry... Then he forced himself to swim back slowly, sliding into the shallows until the water no longer covered his body. He rose, dripping, and walked up the beach, leaping from branch to branch to avoid the thorns.

At the beachhead, he looked back. The sea was red, rippling with shadows. Jonah felt a weight of sadness descend on him. He trudged back up the path that threaded through the coconut trees, breadfruit trees, and scrub before scrambling to join the sea road that skirted the edge of the island.

As he walked, the forests rose to his right, tangled and impenetrable, ringing with go-away birds and crickets, to the flat granite peaks of the mountain, wreathed in clouds and backlit by the setting sun.

The road was crowded with foot traffic. Gangs of fishermen in tattered shorts strode past, shouldering rolled-up nets. Housewives and maids hurried home, clutching striped bags or holding packages on their heads with one hand. Everyone walked in silence—none of the usual jokes from the fishermen or the shrill laughter of the women.

A hundred yards on, Jonah reached the village—two ramshackle *boutiques* on one side of the road and an open space of beaten sand on the other, shaded by a spreading Takamaka tree. Until a few months ago, people would gather here to exchange the day's gossip before strolling home for the evening meal, but now the village was deserted. The *boutiques* had long ago closed. A bored Tanzanian militia patrol in loose-fitting fatigues now lay sprawled around the tree, their AK-47 rifles within reach. Jonah's heart thumped and his chest clenched as he passed them. The soldiers had arrived, as the new President had announced over the radio, "To protect the people and the state from the enemies of the Revolution."

One of the soldiers shouted something in Swahili, picked up his rifle, and shook it playfully at Jonah, grinning. Jonah broke into a run, and the soldiers laughed. Once out of sight, he slowed to a walk again. *Perhaps Dad didn't go to sea at all,* he thought. *Perhaps* they *took him away, like the others...* He turned off the road and onto the gravel path leading to the house. As he passed old Monsieur Malforge's place—a shack lost in overgrown banana trees—one of the windows slammed open. The old man's shaggy head emerged.

"Better hurry home, boy!" he roared. "If those demon-soldiers don't eat you up, I certainly will!"

"Yes, Bonhomme!" Jonah called, smiling in spite of himself. His father used to tell him that the Bonhomme finds children who are still awake after bedtime and eats them. *Of course he does*, Jonah thought now, smiling. *And I bet he and Sungula* are the best of friends too.* Those stories brought his father's absence crashing down on him again. He hunched his shoulders and hurried on. The path wound through the vegetation before opening up to reveal a two-story building of white coral blocks with a corrugated roof, nestling among breadfruit trees. Lights shone through the windows, which stood open as always, covered only by net screens so that even the slightest breeze could alleviate the sweltering heat of the day. Inside, Jonah could see his mother at the table, dinner laid out. In spite of his resentment, he wondered what she and Madame Paul had made.

He entered the house through the kitchen door and found Madame

Paul at the sink, scrubbing pots. He watched her for a moment and remembered how she had bathed him as a child while he stood in a tin basin and how her hard, brown hands had flayed his skin like sandpaper.

She looked up and her eyes widened.

"Jonah, your mother is worrying about you! Where you go to?"

"I was coming home," Jonah said. "I told her that. She didn't have to worry."

Madame Paul rested her hands on her hips. "Well she is worrying! You know what happen to people after curfew..."

"It wasn't dark yet!" Jonah protested.

Madame Paul turned back to the sink. "Well," she said in the resigned voice he knew so well, "go in then."

Jonah took a deep breath and made for the table without looking at his mother, but before he could sit down, she laid down her fork and spoke:

"Don't you dare sit down at my table."

Jonah stopped. It was his favorite meal—dry-fried mackerel with rice and fried plantains.

"If you can't show me the respect of an adult conversation," she continued, "you can't eat my food."

Jonah's mouth flooded with saliva. "I'm sorry, Mum."

His mother was silent for a long moment, looking at him.

"All right," she sighed, gesturing to a chair. "Let's try again."

Jonah sat and looked down at his hands.

"Madame Paul!" his mother called. Madame Paul appeared in the kitchen doorway, drying her hands.

"I will clear up. You can go if you want."

"I can do it, Madame—"

"No, no, you go home. It's dark, and I'm worried about the patrols."

"Huh!" Madame Paul clicked her tongue. "Those army cowards are never leaving the road after sunset. But if you insist..."

"Absolutely," Jonah's mother nodded. "Go."

"Good. Good night, Madame! Good night, Jonah!"

13

"Good night, Madame Paul."

" 'Night Madame Paul," Jonah mumbled.

Madame Paul disappeared back into the kitchen. A minute later, the back door slammed and her footsteps lumbered away through the grass.

"I know what you think, Jonah," his mother said. "You think that because I accepted Harry's offer, I gave up on your father, stopped loving him—and somehow, by extension, you too. Is that true?"

Jonah shrugged, but he did not look up. He felt numb.

"Now I could just tell you that it's not true, but that wouldn't help. So I'll tell you a story. You know that your ancestor, my great-great-grandmother, came to these islands on the first ship."

Jonah nodded. He knew the story by heart.

"When she came," his mother continued, "there was no one here. It was an empty paradise, and she should have been free to build a life along with the other settlers. But she and others like her were not free. They wore chains, and the *grandblancs* who owned the plantations made them cut cinnamon bark and coconuts all day long and kept them penned up like donkeys. When she was too old to be productive, they freed her. But she and her descendants remained poor, the plantation owners made sure of that. I grew up barefoot and eating nothing but—"

"Breadfruit and fish," Jonah sighed. "I know."

His mother touched his arm.

"Yes, but listen. I met your father. He was the son of grandblanc, educated by the Jesuit fathers. He had even been sent to England to attend University College and become a lawyer. But he fell in love with me, a poor girl, and he married me against his father's wishes. He sold his firm to buy his boat. And now I will tell you what you don't know. Your granddad cut him off for that."

"Cut him off?" Jonah frowned.

"His inheritance, land, everything. Your father gave it all up. For me."

Jonah felt tears gather behind his eyes.

"Then these revolutionaries came, preaching freedom and equality for people like me. And what happened? They've become just another set of tyrants, and we are still slaves, of a different kind. Your father tried to resist what happened. They wanted his business, and he refused to sell, so they blocked and frustrated him, and he lost business to state-owned companies.

"Men were here every day with offers and threats. Your father turned them away from the door, but he had to borrow from the bank to keep the *Integrity*. In his stubbornness, he dug himself into debt, deeper and deeper. Too late, I woke up and discovered what was going on. I tried to explain to your father that, rich or poor, we are all free in what we have, little or much as it is. Only what is *here* matters, what is in front of us *now*. Looking for anything else is the real slavery. I tried to explain this to him, but he thought he could fix everything by effort. Stubborn and idealistic, just like you." She reached out and stroked Jonah's chin.

"So, do you understand? I loved your father, and I still love him, wherever he is..." She took a deep breath before continuing. "But Jonah, you must listen." Jonah looked up and met her eyes. "I can't go on following this stubborn foolishness of his. That's why I had to sell. You have me, and I have you, and we have this place, here and now. That has to be enough. All right?"

Jonah looked down. "All right."

She nodded and smiled. "Good. Now, our food is probably cold. Do you want to say the blessing?"

They ate and cleaned up in silence.

"And now, time for bed?" his mother asked.

"Yes. Good night," Jonah replied. He kissed her on the cheek, but he could not bring himself to look into her eyes.

"Good night, my love."

He climbed the stairs, collapsed on his bed, and lay there for the rest of the evening, feeling lonelier than ever. At last, he heard his mother on the stairs and turned to face the window. He heard the door open and the rustling of her feet on the tiled floor. Then her hair brushed his cheek, and he smelled the lilacs in her perfume. She kissed him and

15

pulled the sheet over him, as she had done every night since he was very young. Her footsteps retreated, and the door clicked shut, leaving only the sounds of house cooling, the racket of crickets, and the squeak of fruit bats.

Jonah lay awake for a long time, listening for his mother's weeping in the next room. He had relied on that sound to help him to fall asleep. Now she was silent, and he was sleepless. He switched on his bedside lamp and read *Tintin* comics until physical exhaustion dropped him into a restless sleep.

Moonlight crept across the floor and touched the edge of Jonah's bed. Jonah tossed in his sleep, as if aware of being watched. Then the moonlight shivered and formed itself into a pale, round-faced man with dark, worried eyes.

Malach the Djinn looked down at Jonah. Ever since Lord Geist has assigned him this task, he had glimpsed an opportunity. Somewhere, just below the surface...

The Elder said that this one would defeat Lord Geist. Only Lord Geist... And he was afraid too, as if the boy could really succeed... Then Malach's face broke into a smile. *If the boy is Lord Geist's enemy, then perhaps he may be my friend. If he does succeed, and Lord Geist is defeated, perhaps I can make that defeat into my victory... Get the old rogue out the door at last...*

He worked over his plan for several minutes, testing it for flaws and finding none. He took a deep breath, leaned down, and murmured into the ear of the sleeping boy, "Jonah! Son, wake up. It's me, it's Dad!"

*The ancestor of Brer Rabbit who figures in many African and Creole legends.

16

3

Chapter Three

J onah struggled to the surface of sleep. He had dreamed that he was sailing his dinghy, *Albatross,* across a still ocean. His father had been running beside him on the water, encouraging him and offering advice—*watch the tell-tales, pull up a little, that's it, now tighten the sheet to compensate, that's it.*

And then the boat had gone over, and Jonah was in the water, drifting down through the sunbeams toward the receding ocean floor. Beside him, his father smiled at Jonah's fear of the depths, and Jonah knew then that his father was dead in the dream too, not just in real life.

Suddenly, he felt as if a claw had raked his lungs, and he knew he was drowning. He kicked and pulled himself up. But his father went on sinking, his face expressionless as he watched Jonah rise.

Then Jonah broke into the air and woke in his moonlit bedroom.

Seeing the boy open his eyes, Malach drew back. A human touch could strip away his disguise. He could not risk the boy exposing his real nature. Not yet.

"Dad!" Jonah murmured. "I thought you drowned!"

Malach, thinking on his feet, threw his arms wide. "No, son. I am alive. But I am lost, and I need your help!"

"I know," Jonah said, yawning.

"Know what?" Malach asked. *How on earth can he know...?*

"You want me to take care of Mum," Jonah said, and closed his eyes.

"No!" The Djinn shook his head. *This is not going the right way at all.* "Of course you should take care of her, but..." he stumbled, "I'm alive, you see..."

"She doesn't understand. She wants me to forget you."

What to say, what to say! "I'm sure she loves you."

"Maybe," Jonah said. "She just doesn't understand."

Damn! Malach thought. *He's falling asleep again!* He came as close to Jonah as he dared without touching, and hissed, "Jonah! Wake up! I have something to tell you... I'm really alive, son!"

"I knew you were," Jonah murmured. "You always were. You taught me how to sail. I loved that."

"Yes, yes," the Djinn said, shaking with impatience. "Listen, I need help!"

"I'd like to help, Dad..."

"You can!" Malach almost shouted. *At last,* he thought. *At last...*

"I could help sail your ship. But you'd never let me."

Malach's shoulders sagged. *Maybe Lord Geist was right. I'm not up to this.*

"You are much too young to sail my ship," he said, without thinking.

Jonah opened his eyes and sat up.

"That's not what you said! You said that Mum was the one who was scared of me going out on the water!"

Malach floated backwards, surprised. *That woke him up! Perhaps I'll push on this button a little.*

"That too," he said slowly. "But Jonah, you are only fourteen, and..."

Jonah kicked his feet in indignation. "You said that ocean sailing was no different than sailing *Albatross*, only bigger..."

"Except that you're on the open ocean, don't forget," Malach added, thinking, *I've got it, by the Wind! I've got it!*

"So what? I can handle it!"

"Really? You think so?"

"Of course!" Jonah slapped the sheet. "You said so too, more than once! You said it was just Mum."

"Well," Malach tilted his head. "She worries about you."

"She thinks I'm a baby, and I'm not!"

The apparition of his father nodded in sympathy.

"You're grown up now."

"Yes!"

"You can make your own decisions, you can take action..."

"Of course I can!"

The Djinn chuckled to himself. *Too easy!*

"Then perhaps you need to show her, Jonah," he said.

"I want to, but I don't know how..."

Jonah twisted the sheet around his hand and looked out the window. Moonlight flickering on the water...

"Let me ask you," the Djinn said. "Do you believe that I died? Do you really believe it?"

Jonah's eyes filled with tears. "No, Dad. I never believed it. Except tonight, I was starting to when Mum told me—"

"Of course she did! *She* wants to get on with her life! You can't blame her for that. But *you* don't believe it, and you can't let her change your mind. After all, what evidence does she have that you don't?"

"What do you mean?" Jonah frowned.

"She thinks I am dead. But how does she really know?"

"She doesn't, I suppose..."

"You see?" the Djinn said. "The only difference is that she doesn't believe and you do, and you need to show her that you are old enough to make up your own mind."

"But how do I do that?" Jonah said. "I can't convince her..."

"Not with words you can't," Malach shook his head. "*Actions* are all that matter in the end."

"What kind of actions?" Jonah said, leaning forward. Malach could see that he was truly awake.

This is it, Malach though. He took a deep breath and plunged in. "Like taking *Albatross* out and coming to find me."

Jonah stared at him. "But I don't know where you went."

"You know that island that lies opposite us?"

"You mean Isle Decouvre."

"Yes. You know who lives there?"

Jonah nodded. "Captain Aquille. The hermit." All he knew about the Captain was that, two days a week, a small boat from the main island carried a supply of tea, bread, and other staples to him. Included in the delivery were the latest copies of *The Times of London* in plastic bags. The pilot of the boat left his delivery above the high tide mark, and he had never seen the Captain. Rumor had it that the hermit came from Zanzibar. One story even had it that he was the last living descendent of those unknown Arab sailors whose grave-markers were left on the north shore long before the first settlers arrived.

"What does he know about anything?" Jonah said. "He's crazy."

"He will show you the lamp to light your path," the apparition said. "Do exactly what he says, Jonah."

"But how would he know?" Jonah frowned. "Who are you?" he demanded, blinking. "Are you really my Dad?" He reached out toward Malach, and the Djinn floated backwards out of reach.

"I'm just a dream, Jonah," he whispered. "But some dreams are more real than life. Come and find me."

"But where are you?" Jonah said.

"The hidden island," Malach said. "Just tell the old man. He knows where it is."

Jonah was uncertain. "What shall I tell Mum?"

Malach barely restrained his impatience. "Do you need to tell her anything?"

"Well..." Jonah frowned. "She'll be upset, won't she?"

What an idiot I am, Malach thought. *Of course she will! Think carefully now...*

"Yes she will," he said. "But if you tell her, she will almost certainly stop you from going."

Jonah was silent, seeing the dilemma. "You're right. She won't believe me."

"No," the Djinn said with evident relief. "No, she won't."

"But I can't just take off!" Jonah said, with a note of pleading.

"Write her a note," Malach suggested. "Tell her not to worry, that you are old enough to take responsibility."

"I suppose..." Jonah whispered, looking down at his hands, as Malach delivered the *coup-de-grace*.

"Jonah, one day, this will all be over. We'll all be together again, just as we were."

Jonah said nothing, but tears pricked at the back of his eyes.

"You thought that would never happen, didn't you?" Malach said. "You thought I would never come back. You thought that your mother would sell *Integrity*, perhaps get married again..."

Jonah thought of Harry Payet holding his mother's hand, and he clenched his jaw.

"Well," the Djinn continued. "If you don't want that to happen, you must act now. It is a risk, but..."

"All right," Jonah whispered.

Malach smiled. *My Elder Lord, prepare for your defeat!*

"Good," he said. "And remember, only the Captain can guide you. Believe no one else."

"Like who?" Jonah frowned.

"Oh, no one in particular..." Malach said, adding in his head: *So long as I can convince Lord Geist not to pay you a visit.*

"Goodbye, my son." Malach flickered and faded into the moonlight.

Jonah stared at the place where the apparition had stood. What had he just seen? He knew he was awake, especially toward the end, but why did Dad call himself a dream? Was it a ghost, or something else? What and where was the hidden island? And why would Captain Aquille know about it?

So much, he thought. *So much I just don't know.* But one thing was certain—and he latched onto this thought—he could not ignore what had happened tonight, whatever it was. There was too much doubt about the fate of his father. Speaking to Captain Aquille was the only way to find out the truth. At worst, Jonah would return home to his mother's wrath.

No more thinking, he decided. *Just go.*

He got out of bed and stood, listening, to make sure that his mother was not still moving around in her room. He could hear nothing but the faint tapping of the wind blowing through the coconut fronds. He pulled on a pair of shorts, the plastic sandals he used for walking out to the reef at low tide, and a T-shirt.

He eased the door open. The landing was flooded with moonlight. The air was heavy and still, as if the house were listening. Jonah went to his mother's door and leaned his head close to the keyhole. There was no light or sound within. He was about to move away when he heard a sigh. He waited, listening for movement, but none came. She was sighing in her sleep.

He tiptoed back to his bedroom. At his desk he scribbled a note in one of his school exercise books:

Dear Mum,
I know that Dad is alive, and I am going to find him. I'll be back as soon as I can. Please don't worry. I love you very much.
Jonah

He laid the note on the bed for his mother to find the next day then tiptoed downstairs and into the night. Keeping in the shadows, he ran down the path and along the sea road toward the beach.

4

Chapter Four

A lbatross was Jonah's fourteenth birthday present. She was a twelve-foot dinghy, with a single sail, and a dagger-board and rudder that could be raised or lowered depending on the depth of water.

"She'll dance over the waves at the slightest provocation," Jonah's father told him, as the delivery men rolled *Albatross* off the truck. "But you'll have to watch her in a blow, because she'll go over just as easily. The trick there is to keep an eye on the tell-tales."

"Tell-tales?" Jonah asked, still not quite recovered from the shock of the gift.

"I'll show you," his father assured him. "We can take her out, if you would like."

"*If* I would like?" Jonah exclaimed.

"Are you sure he's ready for this?" Jonah's mother asked.

"Of course I am, Mum!"

"We didn't talk about this, Francis," she said.

"Because I knew you would say this," Jonah's father replied, smiling. "But honestly Liza, it's fine. I was his age when I began, in a schooner no less. This is just for messing about inside the reef—"

"Just inside!" Jonah protested.

"She's not a sea-going vessel, Jonah."

"But that'll be so boring, Dad!"

"Sailing is sailing, Jonah. Only the mood of the water changes. Be grateful. One day, in no time at all, you'll be out on the open ocean, and then you'll wish you were still sailing in the bay."

"Or on dry land!" Jonah's mother said.

Jonah's father shook his head in mock exasperation. "Here, I have something for you." He held out a furled cloth.

"Your pennant!" Jonah said, dangling the green-and-gold triangle from his fingers.

"I had one made just like mine," his father said. "Yours—until you're ready to come with me."

"Huh!" Jonah's mother sniffed.

Over the following year, his father taught him all the basics.

"The most important knot a sailor can learn is the figure of eight bend, because you can tie two ropes together, even if they're different sizes. You take both ends..."

"The wind you feel on your face is the apparent wind. To find the real wind, look at the waves. They always move at right angles to the wind. That's how you can really know..."

"When you come about across the wind, do it firmly. Don't hesitate, don't allow her to lose momentum."

Jonah learned most about the wind—the Southeast and Northwest monsoons and, in between, wind that attacked from all directions. At those times, his father taught him to rely on tell-tales, the threads on the sail whose movements warned of a sudden wind shift. And he learned how to capsize without falling in, perching on the gunwale as she went over, then leaping over onto the dagger-board to right her in a clatter of wet sail and rigging.

Long after his father's lessons, after his mother had given up monitoring him through binoculars, Jonah took *Albatross* out to the reef at the mouth of the bay. As he guided the dinghy to where the waves exploded against the coral, he imagined sailing on through one of the many gaps in the reef. But he always turned back toward the shelter of the bay, feeling something he would never admit to—relief at not having to meet the deep green waters yet.

In the end, sailing meant both deliberate capsizings and moments of exhilaration when the wind was right and the dinghy planed. Mostly he just set the sail with a breeze blowing over the port side, the mainsheet tied so it wouldn't slip, and his fingers resting on the tiller as *Albatross* cut through waves no higher than his hand. Jonah lay with his legs propped against the hull, his head thrown back to see the masthead, where his father's pennant fluttered in the sun.

5

Chapter Five

J onah ran, keeping in the shadows cast by the roadside scrub.
Suddenly, voices floated toward him from ahead. He slipped
into some bushes, just in time—a militia patrol passed by. Jonah
caught a glimpse of their features in the moonlight, shapeless cloth
caps, rifles slung over shoulders, and the acrid stench of old sweat and
tobacco. Then, in a shower of sparks, one of the soldiers flicked his
cigarette toward Jonah. The butt bounced and landed a few feet away,
still glowing. One of the soldiers said something in Swahili—the others
laughed. Ice water flooded Jonah's guts. Had they spotted him? But the
soldiers were shuffling on in that indolent way of theirs, their shapes
and voices fading at last into the night.

Jonah waited for what seemed hours before emerging. He ran the
last few yards until, with immense relief, he recognized the rounded
boulder that marked the turn-off and scrambled down toward the
beach. Between the trees, shadows crisscrossed the moonlit path, so
that he stumbled several times on what was usually familiar terrain.
Above him, the wind tossed the tree-tops back and forth. Wisps of
cloud scudded across the moon. It was the time between monsoons.
He would have to be careful.

He saw dark, glittering water, and then the trees fell back, revealing
the expanse of the bay. Loose sand spilled into his sandals and worked
between his toes, but he did not take off his shoes. Those thorns really

hurt.

He made his way along the beach until he came to two boulders. *Albatross* lay in the space between them, above the high tide mark. The waves hissed in fewer than ten feet from the raised rudder. *Good,* he thought. *Full tide within the hour. The more water between the hull and the reef the better!*

Jonah wetted his finger and tested the wind. Onshore—*For the time being at least.* Trembling with urgency, he hauled the prow around until *Albatross* was facing the water. He unfurled the sail and left it flapping while he unwound the lines. A few minutes later *Albatross* bucked in the breaking waves, her sail fluttering, her rudder swinging.

Jonah dragged the dinghy into the water until the water lapped around his chest. He guided the dinghy forward and leaped in. *Albatross* tipped, almost capsized, and then righted herself. He pushed the daggerboard down two-thirds of the way, lowered the rudder, and breathed out a sigh. Getting off the beach was always the hardest part. Now he only had to catch the wind. He eased the boom toward him while pushing the tiller away. The sail filled with a quiet snap. The boat sailed backward for a moment, then turned away from the wind. Jonah scrambled to port, just in time to balance her as she caught the wind, heeled, and jumped forward on a port tack.

He leaned out to flatten the hull on the water, and *Albatross* picked up speed. Now the waves came at regular intervals under the bow, the wind was steady in his face, and the white sail stretched thirteen feet above him like the wing of a seagull, the green-and-gold pennant fluttering at the masthead.

He was really off!

Several minutes later, still in high spirits, he approached the reef. He could already make out the white line where the waves broke against the coral and the narrow gaps where they flowed on unchecked. He drove *Albatross* forward until she was fewer than thirty meters from the reef, the waves exploding in flashes of moonlit foam, seething for a moment before roaring back into darkness. Jonah bore away from the wind, letting out the sail and lining up the dinghy's bow with a space about five feet wide. When she was in line, he leveled the helm and pulled the dagger-board all the way up. *Albatross* closed the last few meters and darted into the reef.

Then the wind changed direction. The sail fluttered and whipped across. Jonah ducked—the solid wooden boom brushing at his hair—and threw himself to starboard, just in time. The boat rolled, then steadied and slipped through the mouth of the reef.

"Done it!" he shouted at the wind and the waves. In his excitement, he did not see the tell-tales fluttering backward until it was too late. Before he could react, the wind caught the other side of the sail. The boom whipped across. He ducked, but the dinghy was already tipping and capsized over him with a loud slap.

He allowed himself to fall backward, holding his breath as he always did when the dinghy went over. But even as he hit the water, he knew that something was wrong. He was dropping through the water too quickly. *My life jacket! I forgot it at home!* Flailing, he tried to take a breath and sucked in seawater through his nose. He coughed and choked, then clawed at the darkness around him, pulling and kicking against the drag of his clothes and his sandals, unable to locate the surface.

Then, when it seemed that his lungs were tearing apart, he came up under the wet sail. The dinghy was still on her side. Gasping and retching seawater, Jonah paddled out from under the sail and around the boat. The dagger-board and the rudder were still in place! Righting her and getting under way would be easy.

Jonah swam to the dagger-board, reached up, and heaved down on it. Nothing happened. Feeling a slight tightening of panic in his chest, he pulled again, this time lifting himself out of the water. The board gave a little under him, and he pulled himself up once more, grabbing the gunwale with one hand. The dinghy rolled, rising toward him faster and faster until she sat upright, rocking back and forth.

He pulled himself into the dinghy and sat to catch his breath. For the first time, he became aware of the breakers rolling and tossing the hull from side to side. Hot fear flooded through him. He imagined the sea smashing the hull and dragging him down, faster and faster as the water filled his lungs. His dinner lurched, and he realized with a prick of shame that he was seasick. The clouds had reached up and concealed the moon. He could no longer see the island.

The sail luffed as the wind shifted. The boom swung in line with the stern, then into the wind. The rocking grew heavy. Albatross inched back toward the surf exploding on the reef.

Wake up! Jonah shouted to himself. He crawled aft and started to untangle the lines, costing himself precious minutes. Occasionally the sail filled, and Albatross tipped but swung up into the wind without capsizing.

The stern was now a mere fifteen meters away from the reef. *I could go home now*, Jonah thought. *I could probably get back into bed without waking Mum... This is ridiculous! And all because a dream told you to do it? Are you crazy?*

He grasped the tiller and pulled in the mainsheet. The sail snapped full with all the force of the wind, and the dinghy slowed, stopped, and began to sail forward, heeling. Jonah leaned out to counterbalance the wind, trying to flatten the hull, but it was too heavy for him. The lee rail was dragging underwater, and there was nothing he could do to right it.

I'll have to jury-rig her. With desperation clawing at his guts, he pushed the helm over and *Albatross* spun into the wind. The sail collapsed, flapping with a frenzy that filled Jonah with fear. If he could not jury rig her, he was lost.

Jonah stood, grabbed the lower corner of the sail, and unhooked it from the boom. Balancing against the wild rocking of the boat, he reached forward and started to wrap the unhooked sail around the mast—one, two, three times—to make it smaller. He then tried to hook the corner back onto the boom. But every time he tried, the sail filled, and *Albatross* threatened to capsize beneath him. Finally, the boom fell off the mast into the boat, and no matter how hard he tried, Jonah could not reattach it. By this time, the boat was tossing in the backlash of the surf, and Jonah started to feel the wings of panic fluttering around his heart.

There was a grinding sound. The boat slowed and then continued to drift backward. The rudder had brushed on coral. Spurred to action before the thought occurred to him, Jonah grabbed the corner of the sail, using his arm as a makeshift boom. At the same moment, he grabbed the tiller with his other hand and shoved it to break *Albatross* out of the headwind. The sail caught, tearing at Jonah's arm. For a second, *Albatross*'s backward drift speeded up. Then, inches away from grounding on the reef, she spun away, heeling, so that Jonah had to lean his full weight back to hold her upright. With the surf exploding over her bows, *Albatross* flew forward into open ocean. There was no turning back now.

Two hours later, Jonah's arms and legs screamed from the strain of leaning back and holding the sail, and his eyes burned from salt-water spray. His vision blurred and spun. Then his head jerked up with a start—he had fallen asleep, holding out the sail while the wind remained steady. How long had he slept? The moon had come out at last, and just ahead, no more than half a mile away, lay the black shape of Isle Decouvre. At its center shone a triangle of lights.

The pain in Jonah's limbs dissolved. He stretched the sail out as far as he could and steered for the lights. Then the faint noise of breakers floated out to him. A reef lay somewhere ahead, but he saw no breaker-line.

The waves sounded louder, and he realized that the deep water must go right to the shore on this section of the island. Then the boat was rocking and tossing in the surf. Jonah loosened the rudder so that it would come up when it hit the sand. He pulled out the daggerboard and released the sail to its wild flapping. The boat slipped in sideways on the edge of a wave and crunched onto the sand. Jonah leaped into knee-deep water, waded to the bow, and dragged *Albatross* forward, letting it be pushed along by a breaking wave.

Once *Albatross* lay high on the sand, he tied the bow rope around a fallen log above the high tide mark. Only then did he rest, gasping with his back bent and hands resting on his knees. His heartbeats stabbed at him. Light and darkness flickered behind his eyes.

At last, he straightened up. He could see the top of the Captain's house just beyond the high tide line, but he had to take a deep breath to summon the resolve to start walking. After only a few feet, the scrub gave way to open sand, white as eggshell in the moonlight. On either side dense forest crowded. The house now revealed itself as a wooden building set on stilts with a ladder rising to the front door. A warm yellow light shone out of two large windows at the front, while a large hurricane lamp swung from the peak of the eaves.

He started up the ladder, pausing to breathe at each step. Then, with what seemed the last of his strength, he raised his hand and knocked on the door.

6

Chapter Six

As if by a sudden wind, the door swung open. There, outlined, like the moon eclipsing the sun, stood a large man in a dark robe. The silver fringes on his bald head and the tired strands of his beard glinted. A distinct stillness hovered around the old man, as if he were listening to the movement of the wind.

"Now what is a boy doing here at this hour?" he said.

All the explanations and reasons drained out of Jonah, and he was left only with the old man's question. *What am I doing here?* he wondered. *I should be at home, asleep... there's school tomorrow, and I didn't even do my homework...*

He opened his mouth. He had to say something. Anything.

"Ca..." he said. "Captain Aq... Aquille?"

"I am he," the old man said, raising his eyebrows. "What do you want?"

"My father..." was all Jonah could get out.

"Your father," Captain Aquille repeated. "And who is your father, and why would he let you out this late, hmm? Tell me quickly. I was just about to go to bed!"

"I'm sorry, sir," Jonah said. To his shame, he could feel tears pricking his eyes.

The Captain swatted his apology away. "Don't be sorry. Just tell me why you're here so I can get some sleep, that's all!"

Jonah took a deep breath and forced his tears back.

"My father, Francis Comfait. He's lost."

Although the old man said nothing, Jonah thought that the stillness in his face suddenly intensified.

"I heard," he said. "I couldn't come to the memorial service—"

"Yes, but he's not dead," Jonah stuttered. "He's just lost in... He's on the hidden island."

Captain Aquille registered no surprise. "Who told you that?"

Jonah's heart thumped. *Is there something to all this?* "I saw him. I was awake, but he said he was a dream."

The old man looked away, and he was silent for so long that Jonah felt compelled to speak again.

"And... he told me that I should come to you and you would help me find him."

Captain Aquille raised his eyebrows. "Oh, he did, did he?"

"Yes."

"Huh," the old man said, and then was silent again.

"So," Jonah asked at last, "will you?"

"Will I what?"

"Will you help me?" Panic fluttered in Jonah's chest.

"I don't know," the old man said. "First we must get certain facts quite clear. Now." He brought his face close to Jonah's. His skin was the color of milky tea and his eyes were both sad and smiling. "You say your father is *lost* on the hidden island."

"Yes."

"Hm. That's interesting. Now tell me, my boy, did you notice anything strange about your father's behavior before he left? Anything he said to you or to your mother?"

"Not really..." Jonah said. "Though he did seem a little... sad."

"Oh? How?"

"The evening before," Jonah said, "me and Mum and Dad went down to the beach. We picked shells and skimmed stones. It was nice. Then we built a sandcastle and watched the tide break it down, and Dad had a sad look in his eyes. He didn't talk much on the way home. The next morning, I heard the car start up in front. I ran out, and he was already backing down the driveway. He didn't seem happy to see me..." Jonah's voice trailed away. "He said he was going on a quick fishing trip, that he would be back by evening, but he never came back..."

The Captain was silent. Then he nodded. "I see." He hesitated a moment before continuing. "Jonah, I have to be completely honest with you."

"Yes? What?"

"From what you have told me, I believe that your father was not lost. He has chosen to serve the Djinn."

Suddenly, exhaustion filled Jonah's his limbs and head like liquid concrete. "What do you mean?"

"You see, my boy, the hidden island is the lair of the Djinn." Seeing Jonah's confusion, he explained. "The Djinn are demons. Their goal is to enslave humans. The only way to get near the hidden island, let alone into it, is in their company. They alone have access to it. No one is lost on hidden island, unless they lose their souls there... Which could well be what happened. So, if your father was *lost*, he was lost in the company of a Djinn, and if he was in the company of a Djinn, he was there of his own free will. It is beyond the power of the Djinn to *force* anyone to serve them. They can only tempt people to enter their service, which they do with every trick and lie, but they cannot coerce anyone. Those who succumb to them are willing victims."

"No, he wouldn't do that." Jonah was shaking, his hands clenched. His voice rose, quivering. "He wouldn't just leave us!"

The old man was silent.

"You don't know my father!"

Captain Aquille pursed his lips and looked away into the darkness.

"I suppose that is true!" he said. "Although I thought I did know him..." Then a thought seemed to occur to him. He glanced at Jonah, straightened up, and patted his shoulder.

"Well, my boy," he said. "I am sorry that you wasted your time coming all this way, but I'm unable to help you. The truth is, I have grown far too old for this."

"But—"

"No buts. Go home and take care of your mother. Life can be very sad. Sometimes we lose the ones we love, but if you remember someone well, that's what's important, isn't it? Now off you go..."

With that, Captain Aquille went inside and closed the door behind him. The lights went out, except for the lamp hanging from the eaves.

Jonah stood, stunned. The world began to spin, and he felt like vomiting. He stumbled down the ladder, fell on his knees, and heaved a mouthful of bile onto the sand.

No, he thought. *There has to have been a mistake.* He went back to the door and knocked. "Captain Aquille. Please open the door! I need your help!"

No response. He banged harder.

"Please open the door! You must help us!"

Nothing.

A sudden fury overcame him. He screamed, beating both fists on the door. But the house remained in darkness—made darker by the lonely hurricane lamp, besieged by insects.

At last, Jonah let his hands fall to his sides, panting. He sat down on the top step, and immediately the mosquitoes descended upon him. Jonah ignored their stings. Moments later, he fell asleep.

He woke to the whine of a mosquito in his ear. The air had turned blue. As the sun reached over the horizon, the wind subsided. Jonah raised his head. He could see *Albatross's* sail, flapping idly, the mast tilted slightly. From its top the pennant dangled, fluttering occasionally like a wounded bird.

Jonah tried to stand, but pain pierced his shoulders and arms. He could barely move his arms and legs. So he sat until the air warmed and he was able to stretch his limbs and massage his neck enough to turn his head. At last, he turned to look behind him. The hurricane lamp seemed dimmer now. Stillness had enveloped the house, as if it had been long abandoned, wrapped in silence to defend against time.

His rage had faded. He had offended the old man. Now his father was lost forever.

He thought about sailing home to his mother's relief and fury and the inevitable imprisonment in his room—*for the rest of the decade probably*—where he would read the books he had read so often that he did not have to think about the words, trying to imagine why his father had left them with no intention of returning.

There had to be reasons. That was as certain as his breathing. His father would not just abandon them. Perhaps he had wanted to protect them from the Djinn. Perhaps the Djinn had threatened to do something terrible to Jonah and his mother. That had to be it!

He would take *Albatross* and continue the search without help. He could find food and shelter on the islands. Maybe he would discover the way to the hidden island without a guide and find a way to rescue his father.

He shook off the fingers of self-pity that clutched at his throat and hobbled down the ladder. His mouth was gummy with salt and thirst. Perhaps there was a faucet at the back where he could get a drink before setting out.

He rounded the corner of the house and stopped. In the center of a smooth patch of white sand stood an old-fashioned pump and a stone basin. Captain Aquille squatted beside the basin, his back to Jonah, working the handle as water splashed into an enamel basin. The old man was no longer wearing his dark gown. Instead, a white *kikoi* with chevron patterns encircled his waist. His bare sunburned back was smooth and hairless. Wrinkled folds hung around his waist.

When Captain Aquille turned to go back to the house, a smile split his face. He put down the pan and waved at Jonah with both arms. "What!"

he said. "Still here?" Jonah thought he heard something like relief in the old man's voice.

Jonah kept his voice steady with an effort. "There is a reason my father didn't tell us he was going." *And I think I know what it is.* But something warned him not to tell the Captain. He had the feeling that the old man would just contradict him. "Anyway, I am going to find him. I came to get some water before I go."

"You are looking for a reason," the old man said. "And you may find one before you are done. However, it may not be the reason you want... Will you listen to whatever he has to say?"

"Yes."

"No matter what?"

"Yes."

Captain Aquille scrutinized Jonah. "All right," he said. "I will help you."

Jonah stared at him.

"But why did you refuse last night?"

"Because I wanted to know whether you truly believed what you said—and how much you want this."

"I want it," Jonah said. But even as he met the old man's eyes, he felt doubt flickering.

"Good. Your desire will be tested, believe me! But before that, how about breakfast and some rest? You won't be able to do anything with an exhausted body in the way."

"All right," Jonah said. He could not quite believe this turn of events, but he shuffled to the wooden ladder hanging from the back door.

Captain Aquille gestured him forward. "You first, my boy." Jonah clambered up, his stiffened muscles screaming. When he reached the top, Captain Aquille raised the brimming basin. "Will you hold that for me?" Jonah took the basin, and the old man began to pull himself up the ladder. He stopped halfway, panting, and seemed about to drop back to the sand when Jonah reached forward and pulled him up, gritting his teeth against the pain in his arms.

The old man leaned in the doorway, his face pale. "Thank you," he said at last. "Not as young as I was..." He pointed down the hallway. "The basin goes through the first door on your left."

Jonah grimaced, picked up the pan, and strode down the narrow hallway. The kitchen had a small wood stove in the corner and a plain deal table with two chairs.

The old man told him to put the pan in the sink, then gestured at a chair. "Have a seat. I will make some breakfast."

Captain Aquille spooned loose black tea leaves into a tin kettle, added water, and cooked the mixture on the stove, spooning in sugar before the water boiled. He cut four thick slices of bread and spread them with jam. They ate in silence as the morning light streamed over them from the kitchen window. Jonah had never had tea without milk or bread without butter, but he could not remember anything tasting so good.

Hungry as he was, Jonah was falling asleep before he had finished his last slice.

"Eat up—you need your strength." When Jonah had swallowed the last crust, the old man rose abruptly from the table. "Come and rest for a while. We can talk when you have slept."

Captain Aquille led him across the hallway, into a bedroom even sparser than the kitchen. Its bare walls were stained, and the only furniture was a mattress on which rested a pillow and a sheet. Thick curtains veiled the window. Jonah made out towers of books on the floor like a miniature city and a stifling smell of moldering dust jackets.

Captain Aquille pointed to the mattress. "Make yourself comfortable there. Sleep for as long as you want."

"Thank you, sir."

"You're very welcome." Captain Aquille smiled. And suddenly, Jonah started to like him.

Jonah sat down. He kicked off his sandals and dusted the sand from his feet. The pillow smelled musty. He did not pull the sheet over him. It was too hot.

"Sleep well."

"Captain Aquille?"

"Yes?"

"Where is the hidden island?"

"I wondered when you would ask. It is in Mysterion."

Jonah opened his mouth to ask the next question, but Captain Aquille raised one hand. "No, sleep now. When you wake up, I promise I'll explain everything, including where Mysterion is. Or rather," he corrected himself, "*what* it is. All right?"

"But—"

"Sleep, Jonah. You won't be able to think otherwise."

"All right, all right," Jonah said. Captain Aquille eased the door closed.

If he thinks I'm going to fall asleep—Jonah thought. Then a wave of unconsciousness washed over him.

7

Chapter Seven

When he woke, the light had faded to grey and blue. He felt sticky with sweat, and he still ached, but he could now move his limbs and head with relative ease. He made his way among the tottering piles of books to the door. The hallway overflowed with red light from the setting sun.

A voice came from his right—"I'm in the living room, Jonah. Come and have some dinner."

Jonah made his way down the corridor and into the living room, holding up his hand to block the sun, which was setting in an explosion of colors on the ocean. The room contained a work desk spilling over with papers, more stacks of old books, and dusty towers of *The Times* teetering in the corners. Here too the walls were bare, and Jonah had the sudden impression that Captain Aquille did not really live here, that he was just camping for the day...

The old man was in a rocking chair in the far corner. On a little table beside him rested two steaming bowls and glasses of some clear, glittering liquid. The old man was wearing the black robe, and Jonah thought, *He looks like some kind of monk.* The Captain smiled as if he had heard the thought and gestured to a stool.

"Have some fish stew."

The stew was spicy—Jonah coughed on the chilies—but the fish was fresh and sweet. By the time they finished eating, the sun had set, and the first wave of cool evening air had washed the room. Captain Aquille wiped his mouth with a napkin, belched, and sighed.

"As you can see, Jonah," he said, patting his paunch, "eating is one of my follies. I always resolve to eat less, but I enjoy food far too much. But you don't want to know about my struggles. You want to know how I can help you find Mysterion and your father."

"Yes sir."

"Very well then. Take a look at this." And with the air of a magician presenting a new trick, he reached behind his chair and brought out a strange object. It was a lamp, though larger and more ornate than any lamp Jonah had ever seen. Standing as tall as Captain Aquille's waist, it was metal, with a bulbous top curving to a point, like minarets in illustrations of *The Arabian Nights*. An ornate metal grillwork connected the top and the base. Captain Aquille held the lamp by a circular handle.

He lit a hurricane lamp hanging from the ceiling. As it began to hiss, white light filled the room. Jonah saw now that the odd lamp was made of copper or brass. He could also make out the pattern on the grillwork—around the top flew human forms surrounded with leaf-like patterns that seemed to grow from their skin. On the lower half, fishermen in boats threw nets into a sea full of fish.

"Well," Captain Aquille said. "What do you think?"

"Is it a lamp?"

"Of course it's a lamp!" Captain Aquille settled back in his chair with the air of someone about to tell a story. "A very special lamp. I was given it many years ago.

"When I was a child, I had a dream. It is the first and only one from my childhood that I remember. I was sitting on a very calm ocean, reading a large book covered with dust and markings that I could not interpret. Then I looked up and saw a man with light shining through his skin walking toward me on the water. I thought I knew him. He reminded me somehow of my father. He held out a lamp so small that it fit in the palm of his hand. The man bent over the Lamp and blew on the wick in its center. At once, a light that was also a wind spilled from the Lamp, blowing the dust from the book, and I could understand the words I was reading—"

"What did it say?"

"I don't remember." Captain Aquille shook his head. "I told my mother about the dream, and she said that I would one day learn its meaning. So, I forgot about it. My foster father died of smallpox a few years later, and my mother, in my early teens. I went to work as a carpenter on one of the dhows that sail between Zanzibar and the spice gardens of India.

"On one voyage, we encountered a storm that forced us hundreds of miles off course. After three days, the crew had had enough, and we drew straws to decide who should be sacrificed to the Djinn of storms. One of the cabin boys drew the shortest straw, and they were about to throw him overboard when a kind of madness got a hold of me, and I asked them to throw me instead. So, they did. After all, a sacrifice is a sacrifice. I remember sinking down away from the surface, into the depths. The next thing I knew, I opened my eyes, and I was back on the surface again, gripping a piece of driftwood with one arm, while the other hung onto this Lamp. I clung there for two days until a passing ship took me back to Zanzibar.

"I could not explain what had happened to me. Every night, my dreams were filled with strange visions—cities in the deserts, mountains, forests. Strange, winged creatures of light, and others, like demons..." He shook his head. "It was as if I had lived another lifetime but had forgotten all about it. All I really knew is that I had come back for a reason, and it had to do with the Lamp. So, when I returned to Zanzibar, I hid it but always kept it close, and from that day onward I became its student. I studied ancient languages, all the mythologies and stories of the past—"

"All these books." Jonah gestured around at the stacks.

"Yes," Captain Aquille said. "I travelled, too, trying to find the places I had dreamed about, which faded more and more as time went on. I bought a ship and explored all the islands within a thousand miles of

Zanzibar. Finally, I made these islands my base because they most looked like the vision of one that kept coming back to me in my dreams. An island with a single mountain rising from its center, a forest full of pools at the top...

"But after twenty years, I had found nothing more than hints and shadows. And the dreams became almost impossible to remember. Then, one night, I had the dream, that same dream from my childhood. Again, I was sitting on the ocean, reading the indecipherable book. The man of light was coming toward me on the water. But this time I recognized him. He was me."

"He was *you*?"

"Yes. And when I awoke, I understood why the man of light seemed so familiar in my childhood: I had dreamed about meeting myself—"

"That's crazy," Jonah blurted, before he could stop himself.

Captain Aquille shrugged. "Probably. And I cannot explain it. But at that moment, I knew where I had been when I had drowned. I realized that in some inexplicable way, I had *always* known, ever since my birth, and now I knew it again."

Jonah leaned forward, captivated again.

"So, where was it?"

"Well..." the old man hesitated. "It's not so much *where* it is, as *what* it is, though I suppose there is a certain *whereness* to it too..."

Jonah frowned. "Whereness?" He was beginning to understand why Captain Aquille lived alone.

Captain Aquille paused before replying. "Have you ever had a dream that felt so real you thought you were awake?"

Jonah remembered the dream of sailing *Albatross* and his father running on the water beside him.

"Yes," he said.

Captain Aquille leaned forward and fixed him with his eyes. "Have you ever considered that this," he encompassed everything around them with a sweeping gesture, "is a waking dream, that we're all just buried somewhere, asleep and waiting to wake up and climb out and *live* at last?"

Jonah stared at him. He shook his head. "That's—"

The old man chuckled. "Crazy, I know. But it's true. At least, that's what I believe. You see, I realized that the world I had been to—or woken up into—was the real world that people forgot, because they were so caught up in their own self-deceptions. Their fantasies became their realities, their dreaming became their waking. And so, the real world was hidden from them, at first by their own choice. Now they're just born into it, like it or not. That's why the word *Mysterion* occurred to me, and that's how I think of it now. It means, 'that which is hidden.' And this Lamp is one way for us to find what is hidden. But you have to kindle it first..."

"That's it?" Jonah asked. "You just light the Lamp, and it shows you Mysterion?"

Captain Aquille rocked his head. "Not light it—it's always lit—so much as *kindle* it. With your breath."

"Blow on it, you mean?"

"Yes."

"But that's easy!"

"The blowing part is easy. It's *how* you blow that's difficult."

"How you blow?"

"The breath has to start in the bottom of your heart. And then, very slowly, you let it out through your lungs and your mouth. But you cannot take a breath."

"How long do—?"

"As long as it takes. It's different for everyone."

"But you need to breathe in."

"No. One long breath out."

"But that's impossible!"

"Not impossible, but it does take patience. There are some skills to acquire, but in the end, the steadiness of your will is everything—deciding that you want it more than anything. It took me many years of frustration and patience, but in the end I was able to kindle the Lamp, and I woke up in Mysterion."

"What was it like?"

"I don't remember exactly. There was a journey, like rising into the air. After that, nothing. And whenever I return, it's like waking up from a dream. I remember the whole thing for a few minutes, and I try to hold onto the memory. I've even tried to write it down, but before I can, I forget. All I have is my original memory and the certainty that Mysterion is real, and *this* is just the dream."

"But if you forgot everything, how did you know about the Djinn?"

"I'm not sure." The Captain shrugged. "I know the Djinn are the enemy, and I know they can appear in this world. I think I was allowed to remember that so I could recognize them here."

"Why would you need to do that?"

"It took me a long time to understand that. It was so I could tell others about Mysterion. That was how I met your father." Jonah stiffened. "He was the very first person I told about Mysterion. At the time, he was just a boy, not much older than you are. He worked at the marina, assisting with docking ships and so on. I liked him. He had an enthusiasm about him, putting everything into whatever he was doing, whether it was scrubbing the dock or tying up a ship. That's what got me thinking that he could learn to use the Lamp. I hesitated at first, because of his age. Then I made the decision and hired him as a hand on my ship. I allowed him to discover the Lamp, and, of course, he wanted to know everything. So, I began to teach him.

"We worked hard on the breathing for a long time. I think he was starting to get a little frustrated, but I didn't notice it until it was too late..." The old man's voice trailed away. He shook his head. "When it comes down to it, I'm not really sure what happened. He just lost interest all of a sudden. He started talking about pirate's treasure. I think he heard that old chestnut about Hodoul's lost treasure from one of the fishermen, and that was the end of it..."

Jonah knew the story well. Two hundred years ago, the pirate Jack Hodoul was hanged in the square before the entire population of the colony. Asked if he had any last words, he stepped up, raised his bushy chin, and shouted, "Find my treasure, whoever is able!" According to some versions, he then threw out a piece of gold into the crowd, to prove that the treasure existed, though Jonah had often wondered how he could have done this with his hands tied.

The legend was used to lure tourists—come and search for Hodoul's lost treasure! One Italian millionaire came for a vacation and was so entranced by the story that he returned two years later, convinced that the treasure was buried on Black Parrot Island. As far as Jonah knew, he was still excavating on the north shore, deaf to suggestions that his quest was hopeless.

"Once your father had that treasure on his brain," Captain Aquille continued, "he forgot about the Lamp, Mysterion, everything. He left my ship and went to work for one of those treasure tour operators that fleece tourists. He was hoping, I suppose, to have some part of a great discovery. In the end, he bought out the tour operator and ran his own business. I never heard from him again."

The old man looked down to where his folded hands rested in his lap.

"Perhaps he stopped because..." Jonah spoke after a pause. "You couldn't prove Mysterion really exists, so..."

The Captain shook his head. "I couldn't prove it in a scientific way, no. But he believed, Jonah. He believed as much as I do. He just allowed himself to let it go, as people always seem to do with things they need to have *trust* in. I still had hope for him, though, especially when he renamed his company 'Mysterion Tours.' He had not entirely forgotten, even though he had stopped believing. When you came to me, I had mixed feelings. I was afraid for him in the Djinn's hands, but I have to admit I was also pleased—"

"Pleased!" Jonah frowned. "Why?"

"Because I knew he had discovered Mysterion, albeit in the worst way imaginable."

"So, there is another way to see Mysterion—without the Lamp."

The old man nodded grimly. "I am afraid so. The Djinn possess a magic that allows them to show humans a way of their own devising. They will share it with humans, are eager to do so, but only for a price. Usually slavery. Your father paid that price in exchange for something he wanted."

"What could Dad want, though?" Jonah asked. But even as he spoke, he felt a memory stir. He could not identify it, but it left him feeling uneasy, as if somehow, he knew the answer.

"Whatever it was, he was willing to pay a heavy price for it."

"They must have tricked him," Jonah snapped.

The Captain shrugged. "Maybe. But consciously or not, he made a choice, and you will have to choose as well. The Lamp is the hard way, but the only true way." The old man looked at him in silence. "Well, what is it to be?"

"But how can I choose? I don't know what the other way is like."

"And I pray you never will. Though you may be tempted to take it. All I can do is ask you to trust me and the way I am offering."

Jonah was silent for a long while. At last, he raised his eyes to meet the Captain's. "I trust you. I will learn the Lamp."

"Good." The Captain nodded. "We will begin tomorrow. Right now, we need to find a place to hide your boat. They are probably out looking for you as we speak, and you don't want to be found before you're ready, do you?"

8

Chapter Eight

Lord Geist stood hunched over the pool. Behind him, crowding as close as they dared, the host of the Djinn waited restlessly, hissing and flapping their wings in excitement. As they watched, the pool distended and bulged at one edge. A moment later, it spewed out a puddle, which stretched and coalesced on the black sand until it dried into the form of Malach. Lord Geist waited until his subordinate had recovered his breath and made the requisite bows and praises. The host was silent now, anticipating his fury.

"Where is he?" Lord Geist said at last in a soft voice.

Malach did not lift his head but carefully blanked out his thoughts to keep Lord Geist from guessing the truth. "He had already left to look for his father."

"Is that true? Look at me and tell me that is true."

Malach raised his head, fighting to keep his mind empty and making his eyes as disconsolate as he could.

"No, my lord," he whispered. "The truth is, I couldn't convince him."

Lord Geist lashed out with his claw. Malach screamed and fell face down on the sand. The host tittered in fearful excitement. All had fallen victim to Lord Geist's claws, but that had not dulled their enjoyment at witnessing the punishment of others.

Malach rose and stood with his head bowed.

"He probably saw through your disguise," Lord Geist said, nodding.

"Yes, my lord."

"That doesn't surprise me. In fact, I expected it."

"You are all-seeing, my lord."

"You had hopes of taking my place. But we can all see—" Lord Geist looked around at the host "—that you do not possess the intellectual qualifications necessary for this position." Laughter rippled through the host. "I shall deal with the child myself. And when I return, I shall deal with you."

Malach was silent.

"I have put Bagat in authority." A short and twisted young Djinn behind Lord Geist squirmed with delight. "He will make sure you do not get into mischief in my absence."

Malach bowed lower, his head almost touching the ground. Lord Geist looked down at him for a moment, satisfaction etched on his pale, bony face. Then he strode into the pool. When he was knee deep, he turned and fixed Malach and the entire host with his stare.

"Remember, my children," he said in a whisper that carried to all of them. "I was present at the Council of Choice. There I was given the rule of the Shaitan, and I shall hold that rule fast unto ages of ages. Let none challenge me, as this one has," he gestured with his chin at Malach, "or they shall suffer, as he undoubtedly shall."

A moment later, Lord Geist vanished. Malach rose, dusting his knees and dabbing at his bleeding head.

"You really got it this time, didn't you, old man?" Bagat squealed. "He's going to fix you!" The rest of the Djinn tittered.

"I don't think he will, young Bagat," Malach replied in a very clear voice. "No, I don't think so at all."

The laughter faded, and the Djinn shifted uncertainly. Bagat scratched his chin and glanced around. "Trying to incite mutiny, are you? I wouldn't try it if I were you..."

"I helped the boy," Malach said. There was silence. "You know that the tyrant prophesied the defeat of Lord Geist at his hands. I decided to help him do that. And do you know why?" There was a horrified silence.

49

"I said, do you know why?"

This is the moment when I win or lose them, he thought.

"No," Bagat finally whispered. "Wh... why?"

"Because if he succeeds," Malach said, "and he may, then our Elder will be destroyed, and we can be free from him at last. Free to live as we want," he raised his voice, "to bow to no one and serve no one but ourselves!" The host fluttered and murmured its approbation. Only Bagat was still uncertain. Malach continued, lowering his voice. "But, if the boy does not succeed, I shall take my punishment, and none but me will be held responsible. Lord Geist will know none of this."

Bagat broke into a smile. "I think our brother Malach has a fine idea if he can make it work!"

"I can," Malach said. "Allow me to explain."

The Djinn host hissed its approval and crowded forward to listen.

9

Chapter Nine

Jonah sat in Captain Aquille's kitchen, looking down into his teacup. The Lamp stood on the table beside him, glinting in the morning light.

"I dreamed about my father last night," he said.

"Oh yes?" Captain Aquille sipped his tea.

"He was hanging from a tree, and when I called for him to come down, he said, 'Don't pick me. I'm not ripe yet.' And you were there too... I asked you for help, but you pointed down, and I saw that you didn't have legs. I screamed at you, and the dream ended..." He looked at Captain Aquille directly. "What does it mean?"

"It means you are afraid," Captain Aquille said.

Jonah frowned. "Of what?"

"Of what the Lamp might show you about your father."

"That again? I told you, my father is a good man."

"I don't doubt that. But your unwillingness to see anything else is preventing you from taking the final step."

"It's just kindling a lamp," Jonah said. "But why does it have to be so difficult?"

"It's worth it. That's all I can say."

"Well, maybe I don't believe in this as much as I thought," Jonah said in a low voice.

The old man looked down and nodded. "Perhaps you are right."

Jonah felt his heart grow heavy inside him. *He wasn't supposed to say that...* "It's just that," he said, trying somehow to excuse what he had said, "I can't stand the thought of Dad, alive—and I can't get to him because I wouldn't try..."

"I know, Jonah."

"Maybe I'm just tired. I can be tired, can't I?"

"Of course." Captain Aquille was silent for a moment. "Maybe it is time to take a break," he said at last. "There's a good beach nearby, over the hill. Go swimming. Then decide what you want to do."

"But I don't want to give up!"

"I'm not suggesting that. But perhaps you need clarity—and focus."

"How will *swimming* help?"

"It's amazing what some time alone will do for you," the old man said, looking at his hands.

"Suppose someone sees me from the water?" Jonah said. "They're looking for me, you know."

"The Wind will hide you from their sight," Captain Aquille said.

Jonah frowned. "What? How could the wind—"

"Trust me, Jonah. Go on and enjoy yourself. We'll continue tomorrow."

Jonah sighed. "Fine. I'll see you later, then."

"Right-oh," Captain Aquille said. He sounded resigned.

Jonah swam the warm, shallow waters inside the reef, diving to the bottom, then floating on the surface and looking up at the clouds that rolled high above him in immense thunderheads.

At noon, he sat in the shade of a coconut tree and tried to eat the sandwich he had packed, but activity hadn't coaxed his hunger back. He just sat, staring out at the reef and an ocean that glittered like polished emeralds.

Nothing's changed, he thought. *Here I am, sitting and waiting, and Dad is out there somewhere. Maybe the Captain's crazy, maybe he dreamed all that Mysterion business.*

Several feet away, a dust devil kicked up sand and dry leaves. Jonah watched it, still buried in his thoughts. *Maybe I should just get going, stop relying on the old man. He can't prove anything...*

The dust devil darted toward Jonah. He broke off his thoughts and held up his hand, squinting as the sand flew into his eyes. Leaves and sand stung his arms and legs. When the wind died, Jonah opened his eyes.

"I am glad to meet you, Master Jonah. My name is Mr. Geist."

"Where did you come from?" Jonah asked as he scrambled to his feet.

"I have been hiding. Like a fly on a wall."

"What do you want from me?"

"I want nothing from you," Mr. Geist replied. "The question is, what do you want from *me*?"

Jonah frowned. "I don't even know you."

"Actually, you do know me, if only vicariously."

"What do you mean?"

Mr. Geist inclined his head. "Do you recognize this?"

He held out a scrap of green-and-gold cloth. Jonah's heart beat painfully in his chest. "The pennant from Dad's ship," he whispered at last.

"Yes," Mr. Geist smiled. "I was the tourist who accompanied him on his last-minute fishing trip."

"And now you're here." Jonah's mind spun.

"Aquille must have told you—I come and go as I please."

With a shock, Jonah understood. "You're a Djinn."

"Congratulations!" Mr. Geist said, clapping his hands politely.

"Where is he?"

"Your father wanted something, and I gave it to him," the Djinn replied. "Now he is in my service, and he will remain there until his debt is paid. So the question is, what will you do to free him?"

53

"Anything."

"Would you serve me to earn your father's freedom?"

Jonah stared at the Djinn.

"You mean, buy your magic?" he said.

"You know about it. Good for the old man. Yes, would you buy my magic?"

"But that doesn't make any sense." Jonah frowned. "Say I bought whatever it was from you and had to become your slave as payment. Why would you release my father? You wouldn't have to!"

Mr. Geist raised his eyebrows. "Clever boy. And you would be right, under ordinary circumstances. However, these are not ordinary circumstances. You see, you are a valuable commodity in Mysterion. You are worth more to me than the mere price of a Djinn's magic. You are also worth your father's freedom. All you have to do is take this, and the contract will be made." Mr. Geist reached into his jacket pocket and pulled out a dark, shapeless stone attached to a chain. He held it out toward Jonah. "You will see your father today, and he will be free."

Jonah stared at the stone. At first, he thought it was a lump of charcoal. But the more he looked, the more the surface seemed to absorb the sunlight, leaving just dullness... An itch of frustrated curiosity crept over him. *It would be so easy*, he thought. *I could free Dad right now and not have to worry about lamps and breathing out without stopping and...* He felt his hands trying to move forward, and it was only with some effort that he kept them still. Somehow he knew that there would be no going back. His father would be free, but he would be lost. He would never see either of his parents again.

He needed time to think.

"So," he said, glancing up at Geist. "This will work better than the Lamp?"

"Instantaneously," the Djinn replied. "You can spend the next twenty years trying to make that Lamp work, or you can have Mysterion now. It is your choice."

Geist glanced away as if he were not interested in Jonah's response, but Jonah could see him watching from the corner of his eyes. That small deception made Jonah hesitate.

"And how long will I have to serve you?"

The Djinn's eyes darted back. "Until your debt is paid," he said, smiling at his own wit.

A voice, hoarse and exhausted, interrupted.

"Why don't you tell him the truth, honorable Djinn?"

Captain Aquille stood several feet away, half-concealed by the trees. He was clutching his left arm, his face gray and dripping with sweat. Over his shoulder was slung a knapsack from the top of which protruded the peak of the Lamp.

"He is perfectly capable of making his own decision," Geist said. The pendant had disappeared, and Geist now rested his hand in his pocket. He was shaking, as if in the grip of some strong emotion.

"I agree," Captain Aquille replied, panting. "But only when he has been given accurate information on which to base them. On that score, I don't think you've been much help."

Jonah looked back and forth between them, speechless.

"You know that I must stay within certain boundaries," Geist said in a tight voice, "and I have." He seemed even paler than before—if that was possible—and his shaking had intensified. By his sides, his hands had balled into tight fists, as if he were getting ready to throw a punch.

"But you have omitted certain details," the Captain said. "Such as the fact that he will lose his soul when you are done with him."

At that moment, Geist's fists sprung open suddenly, as if unleashing something on the Captain. The old man cried out, and collapsed, clutching his heart.

"Captain!" Jonah screamed.

The sunlight around them flickered. A rumbling began, accompanied by an earth tremor that shook the trees and threw Jonah to the ground.

As Captain Aquille groaned in anguish, a sudden rage swept over Jonah. He leaped to his feet and launched himself at the Djinn. He knew it was hopeless, for the Djinn was twice as tall as he was, but he didn't care.

As Jonah flew toward him, Geist backed away, his eyes widening. "Listen to reason, boy. Don't throw this opportunity away!"

But Jonah was already throwing himself into the hardest punch he could manage. As his fist connected with Geist's chest, something extraordinary happened. The Djinn swelled, his clothes tearing and falling away, as his arms bulged with muscles and ox-like horns spread from the side of his head. Only his face retained the same shape and expression, though his skin darkened from ice white to the color of fresh blood.

"Damn you!" Geist whispered, cowering under the sunlight. "You exposed me!"

Then he started glowing as if the light were cooking him, and his fury turned to agony. He shouted something unintelligible and spun like a top. At once, a dust devil roared up, throwing sand in Jonah's eyes. A moment later it died away, leaving a cloud of dust hanging in the air.

Geist had vanished.

"That was a dangerous thing to do," said the faint, ragged voice of Captain Aquille. He was clutching at his chest and panting with the pain.

Jonah knelt down beside him. "What did he do to you?"

"He used his magic... to stop my heart for a moment. Do you understand now what they are?"

Jonah was silent.

"There is only one real way to find Mysterion and your father, Jonah. You must kindle the Lamp, now."

"But..." Jonah stuttered. "I can't—"

"You can," the old man said. "I will help you. Go on. Get it."

Jonah pulled the Lamp from the bag. As he squatted again beside the Captain, his hands were shaking.

"Lower yourself," Captain Aquille whispered.

Jonah obeyed.

"Lower... so your eyes are level with the wick." Jonah did so, crouching uncomfortably until he could see through the ornate grillwork of the Lamp to Captain Aquille's pain-dilated eyes.

"Now blow."

"Wait. What will happen to you? Will you come with me?"

"I will be with you. I have finished what I have to do here."

"What do you mean... ? Are you sure?"

"Yes. Now kindle the Lamp."

Jonah focused and blew slowly into the Lamp without taking an inward breath, as he had practiced many times before.

Perhaps the intensity of the old man's pain washed away all distractions, but as soon as Jonah began to blow, a tiny flame flickered to life in the very center of the Lamp. He blinked in surprise. Then the air in his lungs grew thin, the flow of air from his lips faded, and the flame began to flicker.

"Jonah!" Captain Aquille shouted with surprising strength. "Look at me!"

Jonah met the old man's gaze. He continued blowing, feeling the pain in his chest spread until it was burning through him. Dizzy, he steadied himself on his hands and continued to stare into Captain Aquille's eyes. The Lamp was as bright as a bulb now, and still he continued blowing, not knowing where the breath was coming from, for his lungs had emptied long ago. Around him the island darkened, as if the moon were eclipsing the sun. Only the eyes of Captain Aquille and the flame of the Lamp remained.

And still the Lamp burned brighter.

Then, suddenly, the light that flowed from Captain Aquille's eyes exploded to cover everything in a sheet of fire. Jonah felt himself dissolve into his breathing, unable to stop exhaling. The island stretched and dropped below him. For an instant, the clouds and air and sunlight flashed down past him, and then they too vanished as he was swept upwards and upwards into a river of pure, endless light.

10

Chapter Ten

The shapeless mass of Lord Geist slid out of the pool beside the Tree and began to congeal on the sand. The Djinn flapped down from the stunted trees that edged the clearing and crowded toward him, eager to hear what had happened.

"The first to come within arm's reach will lose his head!" Lord Geist shouted. The host shrunk back, waiting in fearful silence until Lord Geist had finally hardened into his natural form, then bowed to the ground.

Lord Geist stared at them balefully. Malach laughed to himself—*He's trying to think of a way to save face.* Then Lord Geist spoke. "The boy will try to come here on his own," he said. "All we need to do is guide him, and he will be ours."

No one spoke.

"Bagat!" Lord Geist shouted. The younger Djinn shuffled out of the crowd on his knees, his head still bowed. "Stand up!" Lord Geist growled. Bagat rose to his feet but kept his head down.

"I am here, my Lord," he murmured.

"You will go and ensure the boy arrives safely."

Bagat's eyes grew wide. "My Lord! I am honored—"

"Shut up! Do not make yourself known to anyone, or the tyrant may guess our plan. Go immediately!"

Without another word, Lord Geist turned and stalked away. Once he had disappeared through the twisted black trees of the forest, Malach gestured to Bagat, who sidled up, trying to look casual.

Are you ready, my brother? Malach spoke into Bagat's mind. Bagat's eyes widened and looked around as if wondering where the voice was coming from. Then he looked at Malach with open awe.

"You have the power!"

"Of course, my brother," Malach replied, casually lowering his head and stroking his horns. "All who wish to be Elder must possess it. Geist does not know of my abilities. But he will learn."

"Teach me too."

"In time, in time," Malach patted his shoulder. "I will see how you do with our task and then decide."

"I will not disappoint you, Master," Bagat declared.

"It's a noble task, Bagat." Malach looked at him intently, a fervent light in his red eyes. "This is no mere adventure. It could cost your life."

"I am ready," Bagat whispered, shivering with awe.

"Freedom, Bagat," Malach hissed. "Do you know what that means? Freedom for me, for you, and for our brothers." He cast a venomous gaze around the trees where the Djinn host was roosting, hissing among themselves. "We were not made to be slaves. We were not made to squat on the edge of the tyrant's world and wait for a senile old fool to gratify his ego at our expense. We were made to conquer and live at our own pleasure, calling one another 'friend' and 'brother'—"

"Yes, Master!"

"Shh!" Malach said, looking around while noting Bagat's deference. "Do you want to betray us?"

"Sorry, Master," Bagat muttered, lowering his head.

"Now do as you were asked. At the right moment, I will signal, and we will rise up with one accord."

"I will, Master."

"Go then." Malach gestured him away and immersed himself in an inspection of his claws. Bagat collapsed into a bluebottle fly and darted into the dark sky.

11

Chapter Eleven

J onah could feel nothing through his body. Only his consciousness floated up the river of light. Eventually, the river slowed, and his limbs coalesced in a molten fluid, thickening into something like wet clay. He was encased in solid earth. Sand filled his mouth, and his throat burned. He tried to move, but his body was fixed in place by the earth around him. He screamed, but no sound emerged. Instead, he sucked soil into his lungs. His consciousness faded.

Then, dimly, he heard digging. The weight of the earth lightened and loosened. Jonah clawed weakly, gaining some movement, just as someone reached through the remaining soil, grabbed him under his armpits, and dragged him out.

He lay for a while on the ground, coughing up dirt in painful gasps. The air was warm and soft and somehow comforting, although he heard nothing. Perhaps the sand had filled his ears.

His breathing finally eased, though his lungs still burned with a fire that brought on an occasional coughing fit. He cleared out his eyes and ears, sat up to look around, and immediately squinted again. Before him stood a tall bright figure exploding with light. The being seemed to flicker, and its movement suggested that it was floating. Beyond the light it emanated, Jonah was aware of trees, but the creature's brightness and his own blurry vision obscured the details. He rubbed his eyes and concentrated. The person came into focus—a tall, athletic girl hovered one foot above the ground. Her body was covered with wings.

"Are you an angel?"

"Do I look like some sappy human with big eyes, playing the harp?" the girl said. "I am an Angelus. And there's a big difference I can tell you!"

"What's the diff—" Then a fit of coughing seized Jonah, and he bent over double until it passed.

"Angeli are Elementals devoted to air," the Angelus explained. "We appear male or female because humans seem to prefer it that way. We also take names, for the same reason. I'm Azrel."

"Where am I?" he whispered at last.

"This is Mysterion. And you are welcome, whatever *your* name is."

"My name is Jonah."

"Welcome, Jonah," the Angelus said. "Not that you haven't been in Mysterion all along. I suppose I should say, 'Welcome above ground.'"

"The Captain said the Lamp would reveal Mysterion."

"And it did. It revealed that you have in fact been buried all of your life. And now you are *un*buried. Are you ready? We need to get to the Elder."

"The Elder..." Jonah frowned. "You mean Captain Aquille?"

"I've never heard him called that before," Azrel said. "But I suppose he would have to have a Lethes name."

Jonah frowned and shook his head. "Lethes... ?"

"What you were before you were unburied. Ready?"

Jonah looked around. His eyes had adjusted enough for him to realize he was in a forest, and that it was night time. Around him were countless small pools scattered beneath the trees as far as the eye could see.

"Come on," Azrel insisted. She started to float away among the trees. Jonah struggled to his feet and tried to follow, but his legs were so rubbery that they almost landed him back on the sand. By the time he got his footing, Azrel was nothing more than a moving light deep in the moonlit forest.

"Wait!" Jonah shouted, panicking.

The light brightened. Azrel reappeared. "What's your problem? Why are you dawdling? Hurry up!"

"In case you didn't notice, I don't have wings," Jonah said. "Poor human being that I am, stuck with legs—"

"How old are you?"

"Fourteen."

"Well, you move like someone seven times your age."

Jonah shrugged. "Perhaps the weight of my intelligence is slowing me down."

"Ha ha." Azrel rolled her eyes in mock despair. "Well," she sighed. "Excuses aside, you people of Lethes are always rather weak-kneed when you're first unburied. I'll carry you. Get on."

Jonah hesitated.

"What are you waiting for? Get on!"

Jonah came up behind her and gripped her shoulders. The feathers of her skin shivered softly, like handfuls of living birds. He hopped up, feeling foolish and awkward to have his legs wrapped around her fluttering waist.

"Ugh!" Azrel groaned. "You only look like a shrimp!"

"Muscle weighs more than fat."

Azrel laughed. "Glad your mouth is faster than your body."

Azrel set off again, flying at high speed, weaving skillfully among the trees and over the pools, which never seemed to end.

"Seeing Pools." Azrel anticipated the question. "You can see all Mysterion in them if you look long enough."

They were moving so quickly that Jonah could barely make out the sights reflected in the Pools. Still, he glimpsed a few scenes. Some were ordinary—people going to work, children in school, a family around a table. Others didn't seem to belong in the ordinary world at all. In one, mermaids with hand-held nets herded shoals of fish across a seaweed plain. In another, an eyeless giant dozed under a coconut tree that was the only vegetation of a rocky island. The Phoenix exploded in a cloud of flame before rising from its own ashes with bronze wings spread. A dragon frolicked in the ocean, turning somersaults in the air before landing in an explosion of water.

They flew on for several minutes. Finally, Jonah asked, "How big is this forest?"

"It's a strange place," Azrel replied. "Sometimes it takes no more than a few seconds to get out. At other times, it seems that there is more inside it than we can see on the outside... Ah, here we are!"

As she spoke, they shot out of the forest across a narrow strip of grass. Then the land dropped sharply away beneath them, and they were soaring out over an island, as Jonah clung to Azrel in terror.

"Oh, don't be such a baby," Azrel snapped. "I won't let you fall!"

Far below, dim lights dotted among the trees testified to habitations. Ahead, the expanse of the ocean glittered under the brilliant moon. Azrel was turning now, and Jonah saw where they had come from—a forest surrounded by a plateau, resting on the peak of a mountain that rose from the island's center.

They were rushing in toward the plateau. At the edge of the forest from which they had just emerged stood a gazebo, lit inside. A moment later they descended to the gazebo, and Azrel stopped so rapidly that Jonah felt his ribs creak as they pushed against her back.

Still trembling with exhilarated terror, Jonah slid off her back and landed, swaying on his still-weak legs. Slowly, he made his way up the steps and into the gazebo, which was decorated simply with lanterns and vases of flowers. On a table at the center, the now-familiar Lamp stood, gleaming warmly in the lantern light. Beside the table was a red-and-gold couch and, stretched out upon it, an old man...

"Captain Aquille!" Jonah ran forward and fell on his knees to hug the Captain, shocked to see how frail the old man was. His skin was ashen, and the arms that responded to Jonah's embrace could barely hold him.

"I'm sorry," Jonah whispered. "It was my fault."

"No, my boy," the old man murmured. "It had to happen."

Jonah opened his mouth, but the old man held up his hand.

"You did it," he said. "You revealed Mysterion."

"You helped me, Captain..."

"Call him *Sire*," Azrel said.

"What do you mean?" Jonah said, annoyed.

"You should address the Elder by his title," Azrel said.

"It's fine, Azrel," the old man said. "I don't stand on titles. No, Jonah, it was not me. I simply reminded you of what you truly wanted. Now sit." He gestured to a low stool beside the couch. "We don't have much time. Your father is in danger of being lost entirely to the Djinn."

"Lost?" Jonah said, starting to rise. "What do you mean, *lost*?"

The old man reached out one hand. "Sit, sit."

Jonah lowered himself again slowly.

"I mean," the Elder said carefully, "the Djinn are draining him."

"Draining him of what?"

"Of his humanity, his soul..." the Elder paused. "I think I need to start at the beginning, with the Wind."

"In the beginning, the Wind blew a sphere of space and time as the first light shone out, and the dark chaos yielded to them both. The light itself was so pure that it was invisible, so the Wind opened a window itself and let a portion of chaos in. With all its power, the Wind worked that dark material into earth, air, water, and fire—elements that would catch the light's rays and reflect back its hidden colors. Then, joyfully, it combined the elements in uncountable ways to make the world of Mysterion.

"Snow-capped mountains rose toward the sky in the north. Further west and south, the mountains descended to grassy plains, then yielded to swamps, then golden desert sands rolling away in dunes. Further south still, the sands themselves came up against mighty rivers and lush, abundant jungles.

"And between the crescent arms of mountains in the north and jungles in the south was the vast ocean of Mysterion, dotted with countless islands all the way to the Edge in the east, where Okean falls...

"Having formed the land and the water, the Wind shaped every living creature its imagination could conceive. On the same earth, the worm worked its way through the dark soil while the unicorn frolicked in the sun. In the air, the sparrow darted here and there as the Roc hunted its prey and the Phoenix lived and died in an explosion of fire. In the rivers and streams and beneath the waves of the sea, the jellyfish pulsed among the sea-going dragons diving into the depths.

"And so the land and ocean and sky were filled with every fish and bird and animal, for no other reason than that the Wind sought to make the unseen light and its unknowable beauty known.

"But what is beauty without someone to see it? So it was that the Wind opened a second time and fashioned another portion of chaos into two races. One was the race of shape-shifters who could take the form of any element they chose. The Wind made them to proclaim the pure beauty of their chosen element.

"The Angeli chose air and became the messengers of the Wind's purpose in Mysterion. The mermaids devoted their forms to water and the Blind Watchmen to earth. Lastly, the Djinn, who were fierce and proud beings, proclaimed fire to be the purest of the elements and superior above all.

"And then, finally, the Wind made us, the human race. While the shape-shifters devoted themselves only to a single element, we contained all the elements within ourselves. While the Wind made the shape-shifters to uphold the purity of each element, it made us to sum up all the elements, the whole beauty of Mysterion, and proclaim all that was hidden in the light. Moreover, the Wind called us to preside over the shape-shifters, so that they might not fall into division and conflict over their elements but might remain united in peace.

"However, the Djinn hated the status that the Wind had given them.

Why, they demanded, must pure creatures submit to a mixed race? Why should the strongest and fiercest and brightest of the Wind's creatures stand below those in whom the elements had mingled, becoming tainted and corrupt and weak? They swore to subdue all of humanity, and all of Mysterion, under the element of fire.

"The Djinn soon learned that they could not force us to submit to this element. However, they learned that we can be limited and enslaved in other ways. We can listen to our hearts over our minds or our minds over our hearts. We can come to treasure body over soul, or soul over body. We can divide into tribes, preferring our own at the expense of the others. But above all, the Djinn discovered that they could tempt us very easily into preferring our illusions over realities. Thus they learned that if they were clever, they could lead us into forgetting Mysterion as it really is in favor of a world made up of lies and self-deceptions.

"So the Djinn came to us in various forms to divide us, from Mysterion, from each other, and from ourselves. Being shape-shifters, they came hidden in the forms of insects, animals, birds, and even human beings, but they found that dreams were their most effective disguise, the most powerful way to control how we think of the world. So they floated into our minds as subtle, pleasant fantasies in which each of us was absolute king or queen over Mysterion, each commanding the rest according to our slightest whim. And when we woke, we found ourselves unhappy, resentful of our responsibilities to care for others and to listen to and follow the Wind that was the true ruler of Mysterion.

"That was what led to the first Battle of Mysterion. Those who hated the world as it really is—also called the forgetful ones, or *Lethes*—allied themselves with the Djinn, while the rest—a small remnant—sought the protection of the Angeli. For one hundred days, men and women fought by land and sea, Djinn and Angeli by air, but despite their valor, the People of the Wind were defeated.

"The very few remaining scattered in all four directions to live in exile in the outer regions of Mysterion, concealing themselves lest they be found and destroyed. The Angeli, with no one to protect, retreated above the heavens and could do nothing more than keep watch and bear witness as the Lethes and the Djinn overran Mysterion. The Djinn used every growing thing as fuel for their fires, until the land was stripped bare and barren and the waters were brown and gray with loose earth.

"The Lethes, finding their world even more hateful than it was before, spent most of their time sleeping, lost in their fantasies. Eventually, they forgot even the existence of their bodies, which shrank into mere husks, and soon ashes covered them over, while the fires of the Djinn continued to burn and the smoke filled the air and storms raged overhead, returning Mysterion to the chaos in which it began.

"As their dormant bodies shrank, the spirits of the Lethes escaped and floated down to gather at the base of Mysterion. There they mingled, like an ocean, forming into a single collective dream, a shared illusion in which each of them still claimed to be king or queen alone, only now each had to win his or her claim to power against the others. They even multiplied and passed on their illusions to those who came after them. You may call this shared illusion the "real world," but it is only a part of the real world, fragments mistaken for the whole, parts mistaken for the sum. The Lethes who live in it are truly asleep and waiting to be woken to see the world in all dimensions, as it truly is."

12

Chapter Twelve

Jonah suddenly became aware of how raw his eyes felt. He rubbed them with one hand. His mind was so overwhelmed, he couldn't even begin to discern the questions that he knew lurked somewhere beneath.

"It's a lot to take in," the Elder said.

Jonah nodded. "A little much."

"Why don't you get some sleep?" the Elder said.

"But what about finding Dad…"

"There is more you need to know if you are going to be successful in your quest." The old man smiled and added, "Besides, you should never argue with your body. Take it from me, even if you win, it makes you pay in the end. Rest for one more day, and then you can continue your journey. Azrel, show him to the bower." The Elder gripped Jonah's shoulder. "It's good that you are here, finally."

Azrel led Jonah out of the gazebo and a short way into the forest until they reached a place where almond trees and palms had been woven into a living shelter.

"This is where the Elder sleeps," Azrel said.

"But I don't want to take his place."

"You won't. He sleeps on his couch as well. Now sleep. Tomorrow I'll show you around the island and you can meet the People."

"All right," he muttered. "See you in the morning."

Azrel nodded and fluttered upwards.

"Azrel?"

The Angelus paused and looked down at him.

"Thanks for unburying me."

Azrel smiled and nodded. "Always a pleasure to bring one back."

Jonah ducked into the bower, which contained a small bed dressed with purple linens and a silver-cased pillow. He lay down, but before he could wonder what made the pillow so soft, let alone reflect on everything the Elder had told him, a dreamless sleep overcame him.

The next day, Azrel showed Jonah over the Elder's island. There were no formal towns, but houses clustered around the sturdiest trees, standing on impossibly thin bamboo stilts with walls and roofs intricately woven from palm leaves. Beneath the houses, sitting on stools or lying in hammocks, the elderly ate golden apples one slice at a time. When Azrel introduced Jonah, they greeted him with a ragged chorus of, "Welcome home," before returning to their conversations.

"Why did they say that?" Jonah asked.

"Because Mysterion is everyone's real home."

As he followed the Angelus along the worn footpaths, Jonah caught glimpses of rivers where women chatted while waiting for their clothes to dry on the rocks. Children darted by among the shadows of the coconut trees, kicking up sand in their games. Past the trees and white sand was the expanse of the ocean. Far beyond the line of the reef, fishermen stood in slender boats, casting their nets onto the silver surface.

The world as it really is, he thought, remembering the Elder's words from the previous evening.

Later, as the sun descended, Jonah was the guest of honor at a banquet on the beach. Trestle tables had been set up around the edge of a well-trodden clearing among the coconut trees. As the sun set, the people lit lanterns on ropes stretched between the trunks. Nearer the beach, a group of men wrapped gutted and spiced red snappers, lobsters, and crabs in banana leaves, laid them on a bed of coals, then shoveled more white-hot embers over them.

In groups of two or three, people emerged from the trees laden with platters of desserts and salads, placing them on a table to one side before coming forward to greet Jonah with kisses on both his cheeks. When everyone was seated, young girls in flaring, pleated skirts and white blouses brought around jugs of coconut milk and palm wine. Jonah held out his glass for the wine.

"You're too young for that," Azrel said, with an amused smile. Then she held out her own glass to be filled.

"You're not older than me!"

"I am older than you can ever imagine. Besides, I'm an Angelus. The rules don't apply."

"Well whoopee for you," Jonah muttered, allowing the girl to fill his glass with coconut milk.

When everyone's glass was filled, an elderly man with ebony skin and green eyes stood to offer a toast:

"To our absent Elder and his health! And to our newest brother! We welcome you in the Name of the Wind."

"Cheers!" cried the people. "Welcome!"

Jonah felt his face grow hot.

"Say something," Azrel whispered.

Jonah stood awkwardly. He hesitated, then said, "Thank you for receiving me," and sat down, amid a round of applause and clinking glasses.

"Eloquent," Azrel said.

"Shut up, Azrel," Jonah muttered.

Then the men uncovered the cooking pit in clouds of fragrant steam, and the girls who served the wine brought around mountainous platters of fish and seafood, palm-heart salad, and breadfruit fritters. Jonah's irritation at Azrel vanished. Watching the faces of the Elder's people lit by the golden light of the lanterns, his anxiousness of the past weeks receded, and contentment drifted over him. He ate his fill of the most delicious food he had ever tasted. When they brought desserts, he tasted the nougat, decided that it was almost as good as his mother's, and piled his plate full.

After the tables were cleared, men and women formed lines facing partners. Three toothless old men played mandolin, triangle, and drums, while a fourth fiddled and called out instructions to the couples, who shuffled back and forth, hands on hips, circling each other in time to the music.

"We call it the Dance of Circles," Azrel said.

During the third round of the dance, Azrel tapped Jonah's shoulder and gestured at the moon, which was starting to rise.

"We should go," she said. "The Elder is expecting you back."

Jonah started. Despite everything, the beauty and joy of the place had distracted him from the urgency of his mission.

He looked around with a touch of regret. "Shouldn't I say goodbye?"

"No. They cannot know why you are leaving."

Feeling his old anxiety rising, Jonah slipped away from the table and followed the Angelus into the forest. No one seemed to notice their departure, so caught up were they in the fiddler's instructions.

Azrel carried Jonah back up the mountain to the plateau and the Elder's gazebo. Even in the span of one day, the old man had aged—his hair looked like smoke, and his skin had turned the color of parchment.

After Jonah had knelt and greeted him, the Elder asked, "So Jonah, what do you think of the People of the Wind?"

"No one seems afraid," Jonah said. He smiled. "And they love to dance."

"And yet every single one of them was once as you were," the Elder said. "They too were Lethes, buried beneath Mysterion. It took me many years to wake them, bring them back, one at a time."

Jonah considered this. "You said you were drowned and you came here, but you didn't remember how."

"Yes. I later learned that my drowning was the way that I woke up. I was the first of the Lethes to do so."

"He is known as the Self-Waker," Azrel said. "He unburied himself."

The Elder gestured. "I don't really like that title. Besides, I don't think it's quite accurate. I am pretty sure I had some inspiration..." He looked off into the distance. Then he continued. "Anyway, whatever you call it, I was the first to be unburied, and that was just the beginning of my adventures, which I will tell you about one day. For now, all you really need to know is that I eventually found the power that would defeat the Djinn."

The answer flashed into Jonah's mind unbidden. "The Lamp," he said.

Azrel looked surprised, but the Elder smiled as if he had been expecting it.

"Very good. Yes, the Lamp had that power, though I had to learn how to wield it. Once I did, though, the Djinn didn't stand a chance. The power of the Lamp broke their occupation and cast them out. It was not the will of the Wind to destroy them, so they were exiled instead, and a curse was placed upon them. They could no longer freely assume their natural form. Instead, they could only take the forms of insects and pests, though they retained their ability to use their voices, and I am told their natural form is revealed when they are seen in a reflection—"

"I still don't understand that," Azrel said with obvious frustration. "Why allow them to speak at all? All they do is go about whispering lies and temptations, corrupting the weak and tormenting the frail."

The Elder shrugged. "I do not understand everything the Wind wills, Azrel. I just listen and follow as best I can. For now, that is their lot. At least, when they are beyond the barrier of fire." Seeing Jonah's frown, he continued. "Wherever they wish to settle, they must first trace a perimeter of enchanted fire. Inside that perimeter, they can return to their natural form. It's a self-made prison. Or rather, it *was* a prison—"

"They've escaped?" Jonah said. "Is that how they found me before..." he paused, "before I came here?"

The Elder looked at Azrel as if to say, *You see?*

"Yes," he said. "In a manner of speaking. They have found their own way to wake the Lethes, who were after all their former servants. You may remember the Dark Pendant that Lord Geist offered you..."

Jonah nodded, calling back to his mind the stone's darkness that sucked in everything like a hole in space.

"That is their version of the Lamp. Easier, with instant results, but ultimately deadly. The Djinn use it to capture the Lethes and bring them back to Mysterion. Once here, they drain them of their souls—"

"How?" Jonah asked.

"They have their means," the Elder said. "You will see."

Jonah didn't like the sound of that. "You can't tell me any more than that?"

"No," the Elder replied. "You will have to learn for yourself. All I will say now is that the Djinn will use those they have captured and drained to break the curse and invade Mysterion again. Already they have a small army of drained human beings living near their hidden island. I am surprised those poor souls have not killed one another yet, but they have somehow managed to organize themselves into a loosely-knit federation of gangs that they call 'the Brethren.'"

"Which is pretty rich," Azrel interjected. "Since most of them would have no trouble cutting one another's throats at the slightest provocation. We call them *pirates*, which is a better word, I think."

"Probably," the Elder said. "Regardless, their numbers are growing, and your father is in real danger of becoming one of them."

Alarmed, Jonah rose to his feet. "What are we waiting for, then?"

"Yes, you must go," the Elder said. "You needed this day, but now Azrel will guide you to the hidden island. From there, you will have to go forward on your own. How to get through the barrier of fire, and how to free your father—those are yours to discover. I can help in only one way…"

Grimacing at the effort, the Elder sat upright and picked up the Lamp with both hands. He offered it to Jonah.

"Carry this with you. It is the only way to defeat the Djinn."

Jonah looked at the Lamp but didn't reach for it. "How do I use it?" he said.

"Just as you did when you kindled it for the first time," the Elder said. "Except…" he paused. "Just kindling the Lamp will not be enough this time. Something else must be given in addition."

"What is that?"

"It is called Wind-Fire," the Elder said, "and your own efforts are not sufficient to summon it. It is purely a gift of the Wind, and I cannot say whether or not it will choose to give you that gift in the end."

Jonah looked back and forth between the Elder and Azrel.

"That's it then," he said incredulously. "Without the Lamp, I can't defeat the Djinn, but even *with* it, I have no idea if it's going to work?"

"That's right," the Elder said grimly.

Jonah considered for a long moment. Other than the trees rustling in the wind, the crickets chirruping, and the faint strains of music from far below, the plateau was silent, both the Elder and Azrel watching him. Finally, he reached out and took the Lamp from the Elder's hands.

"I've come all this way," he said. "What else is there?"

The Elder's eyes shone with admiration and pride. Then he became businesslike. "Good. And take my bag too—" he gestured to a black knapsack with a drawstring mouth hanging nearby. "To keep it safe."

Carefully, Jonah slipped the Lamp into the knapsack and shouldered the straps.

"Now, it's really time to go," the Elder said.

"Come on," Azrel said wearily. "On you get!"

"Wait," Jonah said. "She's *carrying* me?"

"Not this again," Azrel said, rolling her eyes.

"It's the fastest way," the Elder said. "If you took a boat, you would be too late by the time you got there."

"And believe me," Azrel said, "hauling humans around is well below my pay grade, even if you are the chosen—"

"That's enough!" the Elder cut in, warning Azrel with his eyes. "From both of you. Get on your way."

Jonah knelt and hugged the old man briefly.

"I will be with you," the Elder said. "Listen to the Wind."

"Yes, Sire," Jonah whispered.

"And one more thing."

"Yes."

"Whatever you learn about your father in all this—"

"I know what you think," Jonah said. "And it's not like that."

"Let me finish. Whatever you learn, remember two things. First, love is the key to any prison. Second, love is not really blind. It sees clearly and loves anyway."

"Okay," Jonah said. He wanted to respond that there was nothing more to see about his dad, but he knew the argument would be fruitless. Instead, he said, "If... I don't come back... Will you tell my mother?"

"Don't worry," the Elder said. "I sent her a dream to comfort her. She knows where you are, even if she doesn't understand."

"Come on," Azrel said irritably. "No time for tears!"

"I'm coming!" Jonah cried.

Jonah settled himself on Azrel's back, the Angelus making faces as he did so. As she floated out of the gazebo and into the air, the Elder waved. "Try not to strangle each other before you get there."

"I'll try," Azrel replied. "But no guarantees."

"That's all I can hope for," the Elder said.

***

After they had gone, the old man lay quietly, watching the point of light that was Azrel moving up toward the stars. A moment later, a little girl aged about five or six skipped out of the darkness and into the gazebo. She had been at the celebration, watching Jonah surreptitiously all evening. Now she came over to the Elder's couch and made herself comfortable beside him, cuddling against him in a way that suggested long familiarity and routine.

"Hello, my little inspiration," the Elder said. "Nice party?"

"Very nice," she said. "I like the dancing."

"You always do," the Elder said. Then, after a pause, he asked, "So, what do you think of him?"

"He's scared," she said. "And he's young. Is he the one?"

"I was hoping you would tell *me* that, Shantih," the Elder said.

"Only the Wind knows," Shantih said.

A buzzing broke the quiet. A bluebottle fly had darted into the air, circled the gazebo, and then sped out into the darkness. The sound did not seem to bother Shantih, but the Elder's eyes narrowed.

They know he is coming, he thought. Out loud, he said, "Well then, I suppose all we can do is hope. And trust."

13

Chapter Thirteen

zrel rose swiftly. The island lay spread below them, dotted with the soft lights. The Angelus circled the island once, with Jonah clinging desperately to her shoulders. He was starting to get nauseous and had just decided that Azrel was doing this just to frighten him when she darted upward so quickly that he felt as if he had left his stomach behind.

"What are you doing?" he shouted over the roar of the wind.

"There's something I want to show you," the Angelus said.

Now the dark expanse of the ocean was laid out beneath them. The Elder's Island was a tiny thicket of lights. Jonah could see other lights scattered over the water further out ("Fishermen," Azrel said), but beyond them, the water was an unbroken silver and ebony surface under a gibbous moon that was now directly overhead.

Far below, the bluebottle fly known as Bagat followed in their wake, determined not to lose them. He had overheard the entire conversation between the Elder and Jonah and was already trembling inwardly with excitement at the reward Lord Geist would shower upon him.

Malach thinks he has the lead, but we'll see about that! he thought. His wings hummed as he drove himself on in pursuit of the Angelus, wondering when she was going to level out at last.

And still, Azrel ascended. Jonah could feel the hundreds of wings of her body fluttering, driving them upward, and he wondered if she would shake him off with the intensity of her ascent. Breaking into a cold sweat at the thought of how far he would fall now, he gripped her feathers tighter.

He was about to comment that they were going to run out of air if they went much higher when they swept by something large and bright. Jonah almost relinquished his grip in shock: it was the moon. His mind had barely registered it—and refused to accept it—when the pitted pearl-like sphere was below them, and they were climbing on. Looking back down, Jonah saw the whole of the world that he now knew as Mysterion as an immense moonlit circle.

It was exactly as the Elder's account had described it: a crescent of land encompassing one side, starting with mountains in the north, plains yielding to deserts in the west, and jungles in the south. Within the horns of the crescent was the ocean, with the islands mere freckles that disturbed the metallic surface. The air was cooling rapidly as it rushed over his skin.

His body lurched forward as Azrel slowed her climb.

"Nearly there!" she said.

"Where's *there*?" Jonah said. But even as he asked the question they rose through another barrier, like a reef except with no water. Now Jonah could see a carpet of stars—quiet islands, or flying with streamers trailing behind. Occasional planets, like seagoing vessels, traced the complex pattern of their orbits across the crowded archipelago. Jonah found that his breathing had stopped. He could not feel his lungs working anymore, and yet he was not suffocating.

The roaring of air had also been cut off. Whatever medium they were moving through was a liquefied air, yet somehow lighter too. The only sound was a hissing like the sound of air in a conch.

Below them, Bagat the bluebottle found himself unable to rise higher. He swore and circled in frustration.

Azrel's voice floated back at a conversational volume. "Air-above-the-heavens. Don't panic. If you try to breathe you will get dizzy."

"Al... right..." Jonah gasped, trying to calm his panicked lungs.

The world was spinning already, despite his efforts. His vision had intensified to the point where everything grew blurry and distorted.

"Breathe in, then count to ten and breathe out."

Jonah did as he was told. Slowly, the spinning stopped and dizziness receded as his lungs settled into the new routine.

"I still can't see properly," he said.

"Because you are still *trying* to see," Azrel said. "Stop looking at things. Sit back in your mind and they will come to you."

Jonah practiced her instructions. He relaxed his efforts to look around and allowed his consciousness to settle back as if waiting to fall asleep. As he did so, the world around him snapped into focus. In a single, all-encompassing gaze he took in the vision of Mysterion, like the shield of a giant with the dome of moon and stars and planets resting on top. When they had been flying at the level of the moon, the islands had been in shadow, but now the dome of the stars washed the entire surface of the world in a silver light, and he could see every feature of land, every wave in the water as if it had been etched in metal by the hand of a smithey.

At the awe of it, Jonah breathed out and almost forgot to inhale again.

"Now look up," Azrel said.

Jonah obeyed. A river of gold flowed above him, moving in one direction—West to East, according to the layout of Mysterion beneath him. The more he looked the more it seemed that the water (he didn't know what else to call it) was moving in all directions at once.

"That's the stream of Okean," Azrel said. "It encircles Mysterion. Think of incoming waves around a boulder."

"Mysterion is flat," was all that Jonah could think of to say.

"No," Azrel said. "It only seems flat to you. That's how the Wind brings it to your eyes so that you can bear it. If you were to see as I see—let alone as it really is—you would not survive the experience." She chuckled. "You would probably be turned inside out."

"But if I am not seeing it as it is, then it's a lie, isn't it?"

"Wrong again. You humans and your logic! Just because something is more than it seems doesn't mean that the way it seems is not sufficient for our level of understanding. For your purposes, this is good enough. When you are ready to see more... fully... you will have the ability to do so.

"Now, that is where we came from, the Elder's Island." Azrel pointed.

Jonah found himself focusing in on the island, his vision panning in and expanding until he could make out all the details of its mountain-tops and forests, all silver under the wash of starlight.

"To the East, the habitations of the Solitaries..." Jonah followed Azrel's gesture to take in a scattering of islands, some of them barely the size of small houses. "Now, if you go further, you come to the Edge."

Jonah's eyes ran over miles of water until he arrived at what looked like a waterfall descending in streams from the sky to touch the eastern edge of Mysterion, a solid wall of mist and spray boiling up.

"Now look the other way." Azrel pointed left. Still fascinated with the Edge of Mysterion, Jonah turned reluctantly. His vision traveled toward the western edge of Mysterion, swiftly passing over several islands, most of which seemed deserted under the light of the stars, until he came to rest at a place where, just before the ocean reached the desert, a patch of smoke obscured his vision.

"The hidden island lies in that smoke," Azrel said. "That's your destination."

Jonah looked at her sharply. "What about you?"

"I am an Angelus," Azrel said. "We don't get involved."

"What do you call this then? Taking me all over Mysterion?"

"I call it being an active witness," Azrel said.

"But how am I going to get into the island?" Jonah said. "The Elder said that there was a magic barrier—"

"That's where the mermaids come in," Azrel said. "They may know a way. Speaking of which, we should be going. Dawn is the best time to get the mermaids at home. Hold on!"

She dove toward Mysterion at the same dizzying speed at which she had left it, speeding past the dome of the stars and then the orbit of the moon. A moment later, Jonah felt his lungs working again, laboring to get him the air he needed. He realized he had grown accustomed to almost not breathing at all. And for the first time, he shivered in the cold of the early morning air.

High above, Bagat, who had been zigzagging aimlessly, suddenly caught sight of the Angelus and the boy riding on her back. Relieved but panicking that they had almost eluded him, he darted in pursuit on an intersecting course. Disappointing Malach would be one thing, but if he returned to Lord Geist empty-handed, his life would not be worth the blood of a swatted fly.

14

Chapter Fourteen

Jonah started awake. He sat up and rubbed his eyes with one hand. He didn't remember falling asleep, but he must have done so as soon as Azrel had leveled out on a course toward the Mermaids' island. Now she dropped toward the gold sheet of the ocean as the sun rose behind them.

"We're here," Azrel said. "Mermaid Island."

"What island?" Jonah slurred.

"Down there."

Jonah rubbed his eyes and forced them to focus. Far down through the clear water, near the bottom, floated an island, ringed with white sand and forested with coconut trees that waved slowly in the current.

Mermaids glittering in the sunbeams rose in their hundreds to meet Jonah and Azrel at the surface. None of them resembled the pictures of mermaids that Jonah had seen, and he held his breath in amazement. Their upper bodies formed every color and shape. They had plaited their hair into unlikely sculptures on their heads, while their lower bodies were finned like angelfish, bass, dolphins, sharks, and even the tentacles of an octopus. All wore gold necklaces laced with precious gems, woven silver bangles, and most were also armed with scimitars and javelins. Jonah wondered how they even managed to stop from sinking, let alone swim

"There's Queen Zoë," Azrel pointed.

"Which one?" They all looked like royalty to Jonah.

"The one in front," Azrel replied. "Blue skin. Silver tiara."

Jonah saw her then—a slender mermaid with a gentle, heart-shaped face and the tail of a seahorse. Something about her reminded him of his mother, and sadness washed over him. The mermaids surfaced in an uproar of foam and crowded in to greet them. Azrel hovered just above the water, keeping clear of the splashing with a distasteful and slightly fearful expression.

The mermaids reminded Jonah of the women who came to the beach at dawn to wait for the fishing boats. When the fishing boats back home sped out of the sunrise and up onto the sand, the women jostled each other, shouting bids to the grinning fishermen for the best of the night's catch.

Now the crowd moved aside and Queen Zoë swam forward.

"You are welcome, young Jonah," she said. Her voice sounded like a stream flowing over pebbles.

"Thank you, but how do you know my name?"

"We saw you through our Seeing Pool," Zoë said. "And the Elder spoke your name in our dreams."

Could everyone know about me from those pools? It was an unnerving thought.

"We certainly could use your help, your majesty," Azrel was saying.

"And you shall have it. But first things first. Some breakfast for Jonah, I think."

"Um," Azrel began. "We are in somewhat of a hurry—"

"Nonsense." Zoë dismissed the protest. "The young man has not eaten for a while. Anyone can see he is too thin!"

She clapped her hands. A large, polished clamshell broke the surface, carried on the shoulders of two mermaids. Another brought a low table, set with a mother-of-pearl bowl and a silver goblet, and rested it in the shell.

Zoë invited him with one hand. "Please have a seat, young Jonah."

Relieved to get off his perch, ignoring the Angelus muttering about wastes of time, Jonah slid eagerly from Azrel's back onto the floating shell. He settled himself cross-legged, adjusting his knapsack to make the bulk of the Lamp a little more comfortable.

Queen Zoë turned to Azrel. "Please forgive me, Guardian, for we are unable to offer you acceptable hospitality."

"You will just have to grow wings, I'm afraid," Azrel said with a smile.

The Mermaid Queen's laugh sounded like waves. "We will do that when you learn how to swim." She turned to Jonah. "Please begin, Master Jonah. We have already eaten."

Jonah leaned over the bowl with hungry anticipation. Then his insides turned over. The cup contained an opaque white liquid, and the bowl held a soup of some kind, with pieces of octopus tentacles and prawns and strips of what must be seaweed. It reminded Jonah of a seafood stew his mother had once made, one of the few meals that he did not like of hers. Still, she had made him eat—it had taken him an hour. The eyes of the mermaids were on him as if waiting for his praise. Azrel too was looking at him, her face studiously expressionless.

She's waiting to see if I'll chicken out, Jonah thought.

At that thought, he picked up the silver spoon and began to shovel in the soup. It was cold and salty, and the seafood was raw. Jonah steeled himself and chewed for what seemed like an eternity. Just as he was about to retch, he grabbed the cup and took a large swallow, closing his eyes in anticipation of whale milk or something equally foul. To his delight, it was coconut milk. He took several swallows, gratefully washing the fishy taste from his mouth.

"Very good," he said. "Thank you."

"You don't want more?" the Queen asked, her eyes wide.

Jonah shook his head as slowly and politely as he could manage. "No, no. That was just perfect."

"A growing boy like you?" Azrel chuckled. "Have some more!"

"I'm stuffed," Jonah said, giving her a threatening look.

"Well..." Queen Zoë shrugged. "If you are certain..."

"Yes, thank you," Jonah replied, his stomach aching with hunger.

"Then we will begin immediately, I think," Queen said. "It is a long journey to the Djinn island. And, if you do not mind me asking," she looked at Jonah, "how do you intend to get through the barrier of fire?"

Azrel frowned. "We were hoping your majesty could tell us that."

Queen Zoë shook her head. "The hidden island is well guarded by Djinn magic. We have no way in."

Disappointment drenched Jonah's heart. Hovering nearby, Bagat the bluebottle was racking his brain. Lord Geist had charged him with seeing the boy safely through the barrier of fire. But the boy wasn't one of his servants, not yet anyway. How could he manage this, he wondered.

"I am truly sorry," Queen Zoë said.

"So, only the Djinn can get in or out?" Azrel said.

"And those they permit," Queen Zoë said.

"Who do they permit?" Jonah said.

"Only their slaves, the pirates," Queen Zoë said.

Jonah leaned forward. "Then why don't we find a pirate to help us?"

Both Queen Zoë and Azrel shook their heads.

"They are terrified of their Djinn overlords," Queen Zoë said. "They would never betray them."

Suddenly, the solution occurred to Bagat. He darted in toward the group and buzzed loudly in Jonah's ear. Jonah swiped at him, but he dodged, hovered closer, and whispered, "I know one who did."

Jonah cried out, and swiped again. The fly was gone.

"What is it?" Azrel asked sharply. "Why did you do that?"

"A fly," Jonah said. "It whispered in my ear!"

"What did it say?" Azrel demanded.

"It said, 'I know one who did,'" Jonah said.

"One who did what?" Azrel said.

"I think it meant it knows a pirate who is a traitor," Jonah said.

Azrel and Queen Zoë exchanged a look.

"It was probably a Djinn in disguise," Azrel said. "Chances are, they know of your plan by now. I wouldn't trust anything it said..."

Bagat darted by Azrel's head, whispering, "One of the Blind Watchmen caught him." Azrel swatted and just barely missed him. The fly did not return, buzzing away to vanish in the distance.

"The Blind Watchmen!" Azrel said.

"Who are they?" Jonah asked.

"Giants who guard the perimeter between East and West," Azrel said.

Queen Zoë looked thoughtful. "On that score at least the Djinn is correct. The closest Blind Watchman has had someone captive. It may be a pirate who turned for some reason."

"It would be a first," Azrel said dubiously. She looked at Jonah. "It's your quest. What do we do?"

Jonah looked from Azrel to Queen Zoë, who smiled in a quiet way that reminded him so suddenly and forcefully of his mother that tears came into his eyes. He took a deep breath to steady himself.

"Let's go," he said.

Queen Zoë smiled. "We will lead you there and assist you. The Blind Watchman is suspicious by nature. He will need convincing."

Jonah nodded. "Thank you, your highness." He rose and climbed on Azrel's back. "We will follow your lead."

The mermaids formed up on either side of their Queen and they set off, leading the way, swimming on the surface so they could communicate. They spent the day traveling over the ocean realm of the mermaids. As they went, Queen Zoë pointed out the sights on the seabed. Jonah saw the Plain of Wrecks, where the mermaids had gathered sunken ships of every kind from the corners of Mysterion—Arabian dhows, European square-riggers, flying Dutchmen, schooners, and junks.

"They are from the great battle of Mysterion," Zoe said, "when the servants of the Djinn fought the People of the Wind. We gathered their ships so that those evil days will be remembered in the Higher Mysterion."

"Higher Mysterion?" Jonah said.

"You may recall that it wasn't easy to discover Mysterion," Azrel said.

"No." Jonah's smile was bittersweet. "Not the easiest."

"Well, one day, this," she gestured around, encompassing every-thing, "is all there will be. Everyone will know it and see it, without even having to try. The Lethes will be no more. All will know Mysterion."

They traveled above the Swaying Mountains, tall pillars of soft red coral, through which an army of mermaids swept, driving fish beyond the Mountains to a plain of white sand and seaweed clusters.

"We graze the shoals there before moving them closer to the Elder's island," Zoë said. "Then we herd them into the fishermen's nets."

Past the plains, they saw pairs of seagoing dragons frolicking. They reminded Jonah of golden retrievers with the bodies of serpents. Their stumpy wings propelled them a few feet above the surface before they slapped down, drenching the convoy with spray. In the end, Queen Zoë grew tired of their antics and shooed them away to play a hunting game with a shoal of red snapper.

With the sun setting at their backs, they paused. The Queen's retinue went hunting and returned with several sea cucumbers, crabs, and a red snapper, which they offered to share with Jonah again. His hunger even more intense now than it had been that morning, Jonah accepted the offer and found that he could swallow the raw meat without gagging. His thanks to Queen Zoë was genuine.

She smiled in return. "You are a worthy boy. Most humans never learn to stomach our food. You almost threw up only once!"

Realizing then that she had seen through his little ruse earlier, Jonah blushed.

The Queen laughed. "Your politeness was charming—and unusual for someone your age."

When night came, the mermaids swam onwards, carving brilliant paths of phosphorescence through the waters for Azrel to follow. The moon rose, huge and silver above the horizon, and Jonah found himself thinking about home—the dinner his mother and Madame Paul would have cooked (oh, for a pork stew with mango salad!), the scent of lilacs in her perfume, and his own bed. As sleep overtook him he wondered if she had stopped looking for him yet or if she sat every day at the high tide mark, watching for his sail to rise above the horizon...

I'm sorry, Mum, he thought. *If you can hear me, I'm really sorry.*

How would this end, he wondered. Were the things the Elder told him about his father really true? He had put on a defiant face, but if they were true, if his father had chosen to follow the Djinn... But then why had the Elder sent Jonah to find him? *Love is not blind,* the old man had said. *It sees clearly and loves anyway.* But even if Jonah could free him, would his father want to leave?

These questions were too much, and he abandoned them. He leaned forward.

"I can't sleep," he said to Azrel.

"You shouldn't have to," she replied. "Sleep is a waste of time."

"You don't sleep?"

"Huh!" Azrel sniffed. "Angeli, sleep? Never! We are guardians, always wakeful."

"I like sleeping, especially on weekends."

"How do you know? You're asleep!"

Jonah thought about this for a moment.

"Okay, maybe not the sleeping part," he admitted. "But I like waking up late, and I like going to sleep when I know I don't have to get up for school the next morning."

"You mean you like not worrying about time—deadlines and schedules."

"I suppose. But it's nice just to be quiet sometimes."

"So it's peace you want."

"Perhaps, yes." Jonah nodded. "Just not worrying what's going to happen."

"That was the way all human beings were at the beginning."

"Really?"

"Yes. And, if the Wind blows that way, it will be so again."

"In the Higher Mysterion?"

Azrel smiled. "You learn pretty quickly—*for a boy.*"

"Mouthy and sarcastic—just like a girl!"

Azrel laughed and did a quick somersault, making Jonah gasp and clutch at her.

As the night turned blue, their conversation faded into companionable silence.

In the dawn, Azrel pointed ahead, and Jonah saw a small island. It rose abruptly out of the sea, a perfectly rounded dome slick with algae and crusted with barnacles as if the island had been submerged.

The island's rocks were regularly shaped, six-sided, and fit together perfectly, like a mosaic. The whole thing looked as if a giant hand had simply dropped it from the sky onto a sandbar.

"It looks like—" Jonah started.

"Wait," Azrel said. "Watch."

As the mermaids angled away to pass the sandbar, the island rose and slid forward, propelled by a pair of giant flippers. A rounded head with narrow eyes emerged, stretching out almost half the length of its body. The flippers pulled the whole bulk forward, and the giant turtle dove beneath the surface in an explosion of water.

"Qatala," Azrel explained. "She's shy. And crazy to boot."

Jonah just shook his head in awe.

"Just wait," Azrel warned. "There's more to come."

15

Chapter Fifteen

Beyond Qatala's sandbar, the emptiness of ocean and sky merged into a single, monotonous blue. Just as Jonah concluded that Mysterion must have run out of sights, a series of islands appeared on the horizon, strung out like beads on a necklace and stretching north and south in a rough line as far as Jonah could see. The closest island, toward which they were heading, was little more than a heap of granite boulders and smaller rocks. Apart from a single coconut tree planted at its center, it was totally barren.

High above, flying in a wide circle, Bagat the bluebottle watched them approach.

Well done, my boy, he thought. *Well done!*

As they came closer, Jonah saw several boats lying on the shore, but he could see no sign of their owners.

Azrel murmured, "We must be careful."

Jonah remembered seeing a fleeting glimpse of an island like this one in the Elder's Seeing Pools. "Where is he?"

"Shh. Not so loud. He might—"

But before Azrel could finish, the water in front of them erupted, and the Watchman rose up, dripping. He was as tall as a house, with a square, eyeless face. His body was covered with hair, and he wore only a blackened loin cloth and stank of old sweat and rotting meat.

"Thank the Wind!" the giant rumbled. "Just when I was starting to get the growlies, a snack arrives!"

"Mighty Watchman!" Azrel shouted. "We come at the bidding of the Elder."

"This is a mission of the Wind!" Queen Zoë cried below.

The mermaids had formed up around the Watchman, their javelins at the ready, but he did not seem to notice.

"An Angelus and a host of mermaids! An unlikely combination. And what's that?" He sniffed. "The Angelus carrying a boy on its back! Now I know miracles can happen. Or maybe not!"

"I was commanded to bring him to the hidden island," Azrel said. "He is in search of his father."

"Ha!" the Watchman shouted. Catching a blast of the breath full in the face, Jonah coughed and retched, barely containing his urge to vomit.

"A touching story," the Watchman continued. "But I have a story too. Once there was a little pirate who decided he was going to be a nuisance to the People of the Wind. So he got together with some Djinn friends, and they pretended to be mermaids and Angeli and traveled East to cause trouble—"

"You are wrong!" Azrel said.

"Let me finish!" The Watchman snapped. "When this nasty little pirate had wreaked his havoc, he came back home, hoping that the pirate king would grant him honor and riches. But, alas, it was not to be, for along the way, he met a Watchman who made sure that none of them would disturb the peace of Mysterion ever again!"

And even before he finished speaking, the Watchman had crouched and was leaping up toward Azrel and Jonah in an explosion of white water. Below, the mermaids hurled their javelins, but their missiles lost their target in the confusion of the waves. Azrel, taken off guard, darted upwards so quickly that Jonah was crushed against her back. An instant later, the huge hand whistled just beneath them. The Watchman crashed back into the ocean, roaring, kicking, and swiping around him as the mermaids' javelins rained down on him.

Bagat saw his opportunity. He transformed into a wasp, landed on Jonah's neck, and drove his stinger into him. The boy yelled and swiped at Bagat, losing his balance and tumbling backward. Azrel spun and grabbed for Jonah, but she missed, and Jonah plummeted toward the sea, arms flailing.

He hit the water with a stunning, painful slap. Then he was under. Something grabbed at him, but Jonah slid through, breaking the surface. Something gripped him and lifted him into the air. As he coughed his lungs free of water, he found himself face to face with the Watchman's shaggy, eyeless face.

Azrel's body glittered and darted around in the sunlight. Below, he could hear the mermaids' warlike cries as they attacked the giant's legs. The Watchman paid little attention, swatting at Azrel occasionally as at an annoying mosquito and kicking up waves that repelled the mermaids.

"Retreat!" Queen Zoë finally shouted to her mermaids. Slowly, they backed away, then dived into the depths.

Azrel rose out of Watchman's reach, fluttering back and forth.

"Azrel," Jonah gasped. The Watchman's hands were crushing him. "Help me!"

"I'm sorry, Jonah," Azrel said. "I cannot attack or hurt another creature of the Wind, even to save you."

"Please..." Jonah said.

"I am a guide," Azrel said apologetically. "Nothing more."

"You..." Jonah started, then the Watchman squeezed a little tighter. His vision exploded and turned black.

"If you kill him, you will answer to the Elder!" Azrel said.

"Then you better get a command from him," the Watchman replied. "I don't take orders from you!"

"Fine," Azrel said. "I will. The Wind keep you," she whispered to Jonah, who was now unconscious.

She broke away and streaked in a beam of light heading back to the east.

The Watchman waded slowly back to his island. "A bit of a shrimp, aren't you?" he said, shaking Jonah so his head flopped back and forth. "Well, boy, think about your fate—until it is time for dessert!"

Realizing that Jonah was unconscious, the Watchman stopped shaking him and examined his prize a little more closely. He pulled the knapsack off Jonah's shoulders and removed the Lamp, peering at it between two fingers. "Stolen trinket," he muttered and tossed it away into the water. Then he scrambled up among the rocks until he reached a huge boulder. Rolling it away, he revealed the black mouth of a cave, tossed the boy inside, and began to roll the boulder back.

Above, Bagat panicked, thinking, *If I have to tell Lord Geist that the boy was eaten by a monster—!*

He darted down and zipped into the cave just as the boulder closed the mouth.

Jonah came to, aware of the stench of the Watchman that filled the stifling, humid air around him. Then a hand was shaking his shoulder.

"Wake up, my friend." It was the voice of a young man of about Jonah's age. Jonah tried to see his face, but the darkness was impenetrable.

"Where am I?"

"The man-eater's lair. If the smell wasn't indicating it already."

"And who are you?"

"I am... I was ... one of Hodoul's wards," the boy said.

"Hodoul?" Jonah racked his brain, then remembered. "The pirate!"

"We are calling him the Pirate King."

"So you're a pirate."

"I was one of the Brethren."

"Was?"

"I was leaving. I was tired."

94

"Tired of what?" Jonah heard the boy shift, and the sound of rustling. He wondered if he had offended him. Then the boy spoke.

"Reach out."

Jonah stretched out his hand to touch the boy's back. Immediately, however, he knew there was something wrong. He could feel ridges, like seams in cloth. Most of the ridges were hardened, but a few were still damp.

"I was tired of receiving those," the boy said.

Jonah could not imagine being beaten like that.

"I decided the Elder could not be any worse," the boy continued. "In spite of what they are saying."

"So how did you end up here?"

"This is as far as I got." The boy chuckled. "Not much of an escape. I was fooling old Hodoul into thinking I was still loyal, but I could not convince this monster that I was actually a traitor."

"He didn't believe me either."

"Oh? And where do you come from?"

Jonah hesitated. Could he trust this boy?

"It's all right," the boy said. "You don't have to tell."

"No," Jonah said. "I want to. I came from the East, from the Elder."

"You are betraying him?" the boy sounded cautious.

"No, no. I am looking for my father. He was taken by the Djinn."

"Taken..." the boy said, sounding perplexed. "I have never heard of that. I know people who were selling themselves..."

"Well, he was taken," Jonah said shortly. "I am going to the hidden island to find him and get him back."

The boy sounded shocked now. "Only one with the blood of the Brethren can get into the Overlord's island..."

"Yes," Jonah said. "I was hoping to find someone to help me."

There was a long silence. Jonah had the feeling that the boy was making some kind of decision.

Finally, the boy spoke. "I will provide you with assistance if you assist me to escape. Acceptable?"

"Deal," Jonah said. He couldn't believe how easily this was working out. "My name is Jonah, by the way."

"Sartish," the boy said. They bumped hands and then shook. Sartish's hand was rough and his grip fierce. Jonah wondered what crimes that hand had committed, but he pushed the thought away. Whatever Sartish had been or still was, they were now allies.

"Pleased to meet you, Sartish. So, how can we find a way out of here?"

"I have been here for two days. I know every rock by heart. It's sealed up tighter than..." and the boy made a comparison that Jonah had heard only from the crudest of the fishermen back home.

"So what do we do?" Jonah said, trying to sound casual.

"I have been considering this," Sartish's voice was gloomy. "And so far, nothing. The monster is blind, of course, but his sense of smell is deadly. That's what always did us in on the raids..."

"Raids?"

"Yes, whenever we were trying to raid the People of the Wind, he was always there. The first line of defense, we called him. Even with the wind in our faces, he was sniffing us out every time. Finally, King Hodoul gave it up, and no one has been out this way ever since."

They were silent.

"If his sense of smell is that good," Jonah said, "what chance do we have in this small a space?"

"I don't know..." Sartish said.

Then a flicker of a thought came to Jonah. "Can he tell the difference between us? By smell, I mean?"

"I don't think so. He can tell between humans and other creatures, but—"

"Can you make your voice like mine?"

"How do you mean?"

"Can you make it sound like mine?"

"I think so." Sartish paused. "How's this?" His voice sounded higher.

"Like this," Jonah said.

"Like this," Sartish repeated, a little lower.

"Better. If we practice a little before he comes, it should work."

"*What* should work?"

"My father told me a story once, about Sungula..."

"Who's Sungula?"

"He's a rabbit. A real trickster..."

Sartish snickered. "A *bunny* is going to help us?"

"I know," Jonah said quickly, feeling his face grow hot. "But just listen. It's about a fox, Monsieur Renard, who wanted to catch Sungula and chased him into a hole and put a stone over the mouth to stop him from escaping. Eventually, the fox thought, he would remove the stone, and Sungula would make a break for it, and then he would give him a quick death..." Jonah smiled, remembering how his father told the story, the way he had grinned as if he were a fox thinking about eating a rabbit. "But Sungula had a plan. He had learned to throw his voice to other places, which had served him well when he was stealing vegetables from Monsieur Antoine's garden. So, he said to Monsieur Renard, 'One cannot eat at this time of day. I will come out at dinnertime. Then I will die quickly and you can enjoy your meal properly.'

"The fox, thinking that this sounded very civilized, agreed. He went away and returned at six o'clock when the sun was setting. He moved the stone from the mouth of the hole and peered in, but because it getting dark, he could not see much. 'Come out, little Sungula!' he cried. 'Come out for dinner!' Sungula threw his voice behind Monsieur Renard and called, 'I am out already Monsieur! I freed myself!' Monsieur Renard turned around to see where Sungula was, and the tricky rabbit ran out of the hole and escaped in the darkness. And Monsieur Renard went hungry."

Sartish was silent for a few moments. Somewhere nearby, a fly buzzed, circled the cave, and then settled.

"I see," Sartish said. He gripped at Jonah's shoulder. "It is brilliant. And it *is* requiring two voices!"

"The Watchman will go for one of us pretty quickly," Jonah said. "But if we can confuse him, even for a few seconds... And once we're out, we'll need a quick escape."

"Easy," Sartish said. "We take a boat."

"Too slow. He'd catch us in an instant."

"Don't worry about that. My boat's the fastest in Mysterion. Besides, can you think of a faster way?"

Jonah thought.

"No," he said finally. "If Azrel and the mermaids are gone, I suppose a boat is it."

"You came with mermaids?"

"Yes," Jonah said. He held back saying more. He still wasn't sure about Sartish.

"Very well," Sartish said, after an awkward pause. "Let's practice your plan."

They rehearsed until the sound of shifting rock interrupted them.

"He's coming!" Sartish said.

"Positions!" Jonah hissed. They moved to opposite ends of the cave, facing each other. A moment later, the boulder rolled away from the opening, to be replaced by the square, blank face of the Watchman.

"Dessert time!" The Watchman shouted. "Where are you, my little dessert?" He ducked into the cave.

"Where are you?" The Watchman swung his head from left to right.

"Here I am," Jonah said. The Watchman turned toward him.

"Here I am," Sartish echoed. Jonah was impressed at how similar his voice sounded. Confused, the Watchman turned his head away from Jonah. "What kind of pirate trickery is this?"

Jonah moved along the wall, deeper into the cave. He knew Sartish was at the same moment moving opposite him toward the cave's entrance.

"I'm waiting, Watchman!" Jonah said.

Again the Watchman swung toward him. "Whatever magic you've devised, little dessert, it won't save you!"

"It just did!" Sartish shouted from the entrance.

"Damned pirates!" the Watchman roared and dove forward as Sartish darted out of the cave.

"Are you sure you want that one?" Jonah asked.

The Watchman paused. *Any moment now*, Jonah thought, *he will go for one of us.*

"Of course he does!" Sartish said from outside.

The Watchman stood in the entrance, hesitant. "You think you fooled me. But we'll see who fools who…" And he began to roll the boulder over the entrance.

Jonah panicked. He ran at the entrance but knew he would be too late to get through.

Bagat, who had been watching events from the crevice in the wall, experienced a fresh wave of panic.

Not after all that! He darted out of his hiding place, lit on the Watchman's ear, and stung. The giant roared in pain and swatted at his ear. Bagat flew away, but the Watchman was quick for his size, and the tips of his fingers batted the wasp against the wall. Bagat dropped, stunned for a moment, then darted out of the cave and flew away, his path painfully erratic.

The distraction had given them just enough time. While the giant had been busy with the insect, Jonah had slipped out into the sunlight. As the Watchman turned to give chase, the boys ran in opposite directions, as they had discussed.

"Here we go!" they shouted in unison.

Unable to decide which one to follow, the Watchman stood turning left and right, his face contorted, roaring his frustration.

As he approached the water, Jonah circled along the shoreline, ducking and darting among the abandoned boats. Finally, he met up with Sartish, who was setting sail in a wooden dinghy that reminded Jonah painfully of *Albatross*. Jonah got his first good look at his fellow prisoner—a dark-skinned boy with spiky, oil-black hair and sharp, bright eyes.

"Hurry!" Sartish gestured. "He is discovering we're together."

He was right. The Watchman's head was turning in their direction, finding their scent.

"Help me drag her into the water," Sartish said, a little impatient.

Jonah grabbed the gunwale, and together they pulled the dinghy toward the breaking surf. Jonah could hear the thump of the Watchman's feet as he descended toward them, and rocks began to fall around them.

"Faster," Sartish panted. Jonah tried, but he only succeeded in stubbing his toe. Then the dinghy's bow was into the waves and, a moment later, floating free.

"Climb in," Sartish said. Relieved, Jonah tumbled into the cockpit. His relief was momentary, however, for just as Sartish guided the dinghy out of the wind's eye—

"Now I've got you!"

The Watchman was squatting on a boulder several feet above the beach, facing them. Sartish clambered into the boat, grabbed the tiller, and pulled the mainsheet in. At once the sails filled, and the dinghy leaped forward, heeling in the stiff wind. Jonah scrambled to windward and both boys leaned out to level the dinghy.

The Watchman was wading after them, making surprising speed as the water exploded against his legs. As they left the shallows and entered open ocean, the giant broke into a clumsy dog-paddle that brought him closer with each stroke.

"He's catching up!" Jonah shouted. "We've got to go faster!"

Sartish glanced back at The Watchman, now less than twenty feet away, his mat of hair slicked down over his eyeless features, red and contorted. "We should be skimming by now. There's too much weight!"

"What do we do?" Jonah's chest felt tight with fear.

"I'll bail."

"What do you mean?"

"I'll jump off—to lighten the weight."

"No!"

"There's no other way."

"But I need your help to get into the hidden island!"

"I must go East," Sartish said. "I cannot turn back now. But," he held up his hand to stop Jonah's protest. "I can help."

Sartish reached into his filthy vest and pulled out his dagger. Quickly and without a hesitation, he slashed his palm. As the blood, thick and dark, poured out, Sartish clenched his fist and fumbled around in the bottom of the boat. He found a rag, which he pressed to the wound, soaking it thoroughly.

"You are not needing me," he said. "Just my blood. Hold it through the barrier of fire. Throw it in the Bay of Storms."

"What?" Jonah said, looking back in terror at the enraged face of the Watchman. He would grab the boat in seconds.

"You will understand when you are getting there."

Jonah took the blood-soaked rag.

"Good." Sartish nodded. "Follow the setting sun and the smoke, and you will find it. If you succeed, perhaps we will be meeting again."

Sartish rolled backward and dropped into the ocean, sinking immediately. Unburdened, the dinghy heeled heavily, and Jonah barely had the presence of mind to grab the tiller and the mainsheet, lean out, and stop her from capsizing. The hull came level, and she darted forward just as the Watchman's hand brushed the stern, skimming the waves as the Watchman's roars faded behind.

Jonah sailed for almost an hour toward the descending sun as he tried to sort out his thoughts. His mouth was dry and gummy, and his stomach rumbled. He had eaten nothing since the coconut milk and raw seafood soup the previous evening. When he could no longer stand it, he released the sail, allowing it to flap idly while he searched the hull for something to eat. Finding nothing, he sat heavily, pulled his knees up, and waited for the pain in his guts to recede.

He thought over his adventure. He realized with mild surprise that, in spite of everything, he was utterly focused on what awaited him on the hidden island. Azrel had abandoned him, and now he was alone. But wasn't that the way it had always been? From the day they had towed *Integrity* into the harbor, he was the only one who had believed his father was still alive somewhere. Even his mother had given up. And now he alone had to do what the Elder had called him to do. Whether he succeeded or failed was beside the point. Only the doing of it mattered.

Jonah leaned back. Only then did he realize that something was missing from his back—"The Lamp!"

The Watchman must have taken it when he was unconscious! Jonah scrambled around the boat, searching every corner and compartment, though he knew he would find nothing there. He peered into the water on all sides, as if hoping that the Lamp would be floating somewhere down there. The water was dark and impenetrable, reflecting his own anxious face back at him.

Finally, he collapsed, sobbing. The Elder had told him that if he lost the Lamp, the Djinn would defeat him. Now it was certain.

His father was lost forever.

16

Chapter Sixteen

L ord Geist reclined against the Tree. The sound of Francis's shouting resounded faintly from within. Geist's eyes were closed, and he wore a faint smile as if the agony of the prisoner were a lullaby.

A faint buzzing interrupted the hissing of the Djinn roosting in the trees around the clearing. Lord Geist's eyes snapped open. In the branches, the Djinn stirred, flapped their wings, and then settled into their habitual somnolence. Geist, however, rose to his feet as Bagat exploded into his natural form, bruised and bleeding from the Watchman's blow.

Lord Geist regarded him coldly. "What happened to you?"

"One of the monsters that guard the perimeter of the tyrant's realm tried to take the boy. I aided in his escape, but I paid the price..." Bagat assumed the pained expression of a martyr.

"So he escaped the monster's cave?" Lord Geist asked, unimpressed.

"Yes, my lord," Bagat mumbled with his face in the sand.

"So he is clear now?"

"Yes, my lord," Bagat said. "If he sails without stopping, he should reach here within days. And if the Angelus returns to bear him this way, he may even arrive before the next full moon."

"And you are sure it was Jonah—dark skin, innocent face..."

"Yes."

Lord Geist was silent for a moment. Finally, he smiled. "You have done well, Bagat. You shall receive your due reward."

Bagat sighed with relief and shuffled backward. He found a roost in one of the outlying trees where he could nurse his wounds while watching Lord Geist pace around the clearing. When at last Geist wandered off behind the Tree, Bagat rose from his perch, his wings barely moving, and floated quietly over to Malach, who was pretending to doze on an upper branch of the next tree.

"Good work, my brother," Malach murmured.

"Thank you, Master. Perhaps your thanks can be reflected in the honors of the new order..."

"Of course," Malach smiled. "You shall be second only to me."

"Honors indeed," Bagat said. He was careful to hide the next thought. *We will see about being second...*

"And now what?" he said out loud.

"And now we wait and see if the tyrant's prophecy is correct. If the boy defeats Lord Geist, we must be ready to act and gain control of the cloak and the pendant. Without them, we have no credibility..."

The two continued to talk in whispers. They did not see Lord Geist under their tree, disguised as a shadow, and smiling.

17

Chapter Seventeen

J onah sat slumped in the dinghy. The sun had just set, and the moon, newly risen, was veiled in clouds. Above him, the sail flapped idly in the wind. The boat had been drifting for hours now. The tiller swung aimlessly back and forth as the current pushed her wherever it was going. Jonah couldn't care less. He held the blood-stained rag in both hands, staring at it sightlessly.

His mind was blank with despair. When he attempted to think about what had happened, he couldn't imagine it. Everything he had suffered and struggled through, everything he had done to get this far, and now it had all come down to a certain defeat at the hands of the Djinn. His father, his mother, his life—all lost. Again, the enormity of it rose up like a wave and sucked him into the darkness.

He was so preoccupied that he did not see the light, like a new planet, rising from the eastern horizon. Unlike a planet, it swelled, approaching swiftly until Jonah could not fail to notice it. He lifted his head as the light stopped directly above him, and his face darkened as he recognized the body of light-feathers and the now-familiar smile, both sarcastic and affectionate.

"What are you doing here?" he said.

"As soon as I returned to the Elder, he sent me back," Azrel said. "He saw your escape in the Seeing Pool."

"Why bother?" Jonah said. "If you aren't supposed to help me—"

"I am sick and tired of your whining!" Azrel snapped. "I cannot fight your battles for you, or anyone else's. But I *am* here to give you the help I can, which is to bear you to your destination. Do you want it or not?"

"I lost the Lamp!" Jonah shouted. "The Watchman took it from me!"

Azrel stared at him. For once, she had nothing to say. Jonah looked down again, pressing the bloody rag with his fingers.

Azrel leaned forward. "What is that?"

"The blood of a pirate," Jonah said. "It's supposed to get me into the hidden island, but without the Lamp..."

Azrel was silent. "There's no shame in turning back," she said at last.

Her words galvanized him. He took a deep breath, shook his head, and lifted his head to meet her eyes.

"No," he said. "I have come too far. I must find my father, whatever happens."

Azrel looked at him, and he thought he could make out a glimmering of respect in her face. But as if to put that notion out of his head, she said, "Either the Elder was right about you, or you are the stupidest human being I have ever met." She reached out her hand. "Climb on. We have no time to lose."

When he was secure, Azrel handed him something over her shoulder. It was a little vial. "Here. Drink this."

"What is it?" Jonah said.

"Water from above-the-heavens," Azrel said. "It will strengthen you in the absence of food, drink, and sleep."

The vial contained no more than a few tasteless drops, but they were enough. Jonah felt his hunger and thirst melting away. A new strength flowed into him as if he had just woken from a long night's sleep.

He handed the vial back to Azrel, but she said, "Keep it. It replenishes itself, and you can drink as you need it."

"Thanks, Azrel,"

"Ready?" she said.

"Not really," Jonah said. "But let's go anyway."

Azrel threw up her hands. "Unprepared. Not a chance of success.

Sounds like fun. Hold on tight!"

And then they went speeding west over the glittering surface of the ocean.

Later that night, they flew over the pirates' islands. The largest was a forbidding-looking place, its mountains covered in dense jungles and capped with cloud. Closer to shore were anchored nine ships that looked like the ones he had seen in the Elder's pools—dhows and square-riggers, small fishing boats, and even a junk.

"That's the island of Hodoul," Azrel said. "The others," she gestured at several smaller islands nearby, "are the territories of the Princes. They have alliances with the king, which means that they consent not to kill each other unless they've planned and agreed to do it ahead of time."

As they soared over Hodoul's island, Jonah caught glimpses of smoky fires that illumined squalid shacks. Clusters of human-like shapes brawled and engaged in drunken debauchery in the half-light as the sounds of shouting, screams, and singing rose faintly to their altitude.

Azrel did not linger, and soon the islands fell behind and they were out over open ocean again. Now, however, the quality of both the air and the water had changed. The moon was swollen and orange as if seen through a haze. The ocean below was tinged with an oily sheen. Jonah also became aware of a hint of sulfurous smoke that intensified until the air caught in his throat.

He wrinkled his nose and coughed.

"The smoke from the barrier of fire," Azrel said grimly. "We're almost there."

Fingers of smoke reached out of the darkness to envelop them now. The smoke thickened until Jonah was coughing almost continuously, his hand over his mouth. Forced to slow almost to a walking pace, Azrel felt her way forward, her light no longer able to penetrate the gloom.

Then Jonah heard it—a roar coming from directly ahead. His light-headedness dissolved, leaving his whole body tight with fear. The sound grew louder, interspersed with explosions and hisses.

The billowing curtains of smoke parted to reveal a wall of fire. Green and yellow flames curled and licked the ocean's surface, where the waves broke in a furious hissing. Clouds of steam boiled up, mingling with the smoke to block out even the faintest outline of the moon above.

Azrel came to a standstill, both of them awed in the face of the impassable barrier before them. The smoke overwhelmed Jonah, clawing at his throat and lungs. The skin on his face tightened in the heat, burning more and more intensely. A moment later, he smelled his hair starting to singe.

"Too hot," he gasped.

Azrel backed away a little from the flames, then slowly followed the perimeter of the barrier of fire all the way around. There were no gaps, but part way through their circuit, Jonah pointed. Bobbing on the steaming water almost against the flames was a small black dugout.

"That must be what the pirates use to get in and out," Jonah said hoarsely.

Azrel stopped directly above the canoe. Jonah slid off her back and into the boat, which rocked and almost capsized under him. Swiftly, Jonah sat and brought it under control. Under his hands, the surface of the dugout was slightly sticky. He wondered what substance they had painted it with. Then the answer came to him: *you only need a pirate's blood to get in...*

He felt nauseous, heaved, then controlled his breathing to resist the urge.

He looked up at Azrel. "Are you sure you can't come?"

"Yes," Azrel said. "This magic was made to keep the Djinn inside and everyone else out. You must go on alone."

Jonah nodded. "Yes. I know." He looked down, searching the dugout. There was a paddle, also black and sticky. Breathing heavily to control his disgust, he picked it up. Then he remembered something else.

"The rag," he said. "He said to hold it..." He pulled the rag, now stiff with dried blood, from his pocket, wrapped it around one hand. Then he gripped the paddle again and fixed his eyes on the flames ahead. The heat was beyond intense. He could feel his lungs burning, his eyeballs drying out.

He raised his eyes to Azrel. "If I come back..."

"I will be waiting."

"Thank you," Jonah said. "For everything."

"Don't thank me," Azrel said. "I'm just your ride."

Jonah tried to smile, but he could not manage it. Resolutely, he turned his face back toward the barrier of fire and drove the dugout forward. Almost at once, the inferno washed over him, but instead of the searing heat as his flesh burned, Jonah felt as if his whole body had been encased in ice. The cold seized him, freezing his heart, and his mind became clear and void of emotion.

Then the dugout was through. The barrier's flames vanished, yielding to a monsoon storm that hurled water at him in horizontal shafts that stung his arms and face and forced him to squint. Beneath him, the dugout was completely out of control, at the mercy of the wind's fury, despite Jonah's best efforts with the paddle to keep the bow pointing in one direction.

Finally, he gave up. He focused his thoughts on what Sartish had said. *Throw it in the bay of storms*, he had said.

If it made me cold to hold it, Jonah thought, *then whatever it touches...*

Almost impulsively, he reached his hand over the side and dropped the blood-soaked rag into the water.

The waves died. Only the wind continued to blow, but where it had whipped up whitecaps and green mountains of water, it now swept among frozen crests, blowing trails and spirals of ice that had been foam and water vapor. Beneath him, the dugout was locked in a sheet of ice.

Jonah swung his leg over the side of the dinghy, testing the ice to see if it would hold his weight. It was as solid as granite. He hopped out and inched his way across the ice, hugging himself against the wind that cut through his thin, torn T-shirt. At first, he guessed his direction. Then, between the frozen waves, he glimpsed an island curled on itself like a sleeping lizard.

His limbs stiffening, as if in anticipation of oncoming death, Jonah shuffled toward the hidden island.

18

Chapter Eighteen

A s the Wind would have it, Jonah's arrival had gone unnoticed. The sentry posts on the beaches of the hidden island were deserted, for all the Djinn had been summoned to the central clearing. The clearing was now packed to overflowing with winged bodies, pushing and jostling one another for a better view of the center. Occasional angry explosions of hissing broke out as one of them tried to force its way closer to the Tree, which squatted, immense and twisted, in their midst.

Lord Geist stood in front of the Tree, regarding the gathered host impassively. Only one very familiar with his moods, and standing very close—as both Malach and Bagat happened to be—could perceive his satisfaction, and they now exchanged quick glances of self-congratulation.

Lord Geist raised his claw and the murmuring of the host was silenced.

"My children!" he began. "Our time is coming again!"

The Djinn hissed like wind through fallen leaves.

"Yes. In the beginning, the Wind made us strong and proud, guardians of fire that burns and consumes all. It feeds on the air, it scorches the earth, it turns the water to steam! Ours was the greatest element, and our destiny was to be the masters of all. But then, the Wind faltered and failed us. It made a weak race, by mingling the pure elements, and then dared set those degenerate creatures in authority over us!" Geist continued over the sound of the host's rage. "But we refused to submit. We gathered in the Council of Choice and there you appointed me to set us in our rightful place. And this I did. In a glorious battle, we exiled many of the humans and enslaved many also. And for many years, we ruled over the world, triumphant...

"Then the tyrant came, with his wretched Lamp, and robbed us of our rightful inheritance..." The Djinn hissed louder, but Lord Geist raised his voice. "He burned us with Wind-Fire, cursed us, and sent us into exile. Yet we were strong, we endured, and we will regain what belongs to us!"

At these words, the Djinn emitted a collective howl, which Lord Geist enjoyed for a moment before raising his claw once again. Immediately, the host fell silent. They loved Lord Geist's speeches.

"Since then, we have worked to bring back our former slaves from beneath the world. Our crop has grown slowly—too slowly, as the tyrant himself has stolen them from us one by one to enslave them for himself. And now, he sends one of these slaves of his, a mere boy, whom he believes will destroy everything for which we have worked and crush us down once again!"

The host of Djinn hissed and pounded their feet in disapproval. Lord Geist raised one hand for silence.

"Even now this boy is crossing the bay," he said, "intent on rescuing his father, our latest harvest." He gestured at the Tree. "This, the tyrant hopes, will somehow undo our work..." he sneered, and the host tittered at the joke. "But once again, your devoted leader will protect you from the oppressor. We will make certain that the boy, far from escaping with his precious father, will instead join him in the heart of the Tree. Together, they will feed its roots, and we will feed on its fruit. The tyrant seeks to destroy us? No! He will make us stronger!"

The Djinn roared its approval for several minutes, while Geist looked on with grim approval. Among them, Malach watched him. *He can never have enough praise*, he thought with bitter envy.

Jonah stumbled onto the shores of the hidden island, his arms and legs blue from cold. As he stepped onto the beach, however, he walked into a wall of heat. Within moments, the cold in his limbs vanished.

He took a few steps forward and already felt sluggish. Sweat broke out and ran in rivulets down his forehead. A smell like a sewer rose up at him. He retched, then held his breath and concentrated until he was under control. He looked around. The half-darkness he had encountered at the barrier of fire persisted. The moon was no more than a brighter dullness in the cloud of steam and smoke that cloaked the island. The light that did filter down was blurred somehow, obscuring rather than clarifying what it touched. Jonah could barely discern the outlines of trees and rocks at the head of the beach.

Jonah remembered that The Elder had said the Djinn hated light and loved working in disguise.

This is the perfect land for liars, he thought.

Feeling almost drugged in the damp heat, Jonah made his way up the beach and into the forest of black and twisted trees beyond. As the roar of the bay of storms faded behind him, another sound replaced it, a distant, strident voice that was somehow familiar in the way it pierced and clawed at his ears. It was interspersed with a chorus of hisses that raised goose bumps on his arms. He could not make out the source of the sounds, for the trees ahead tangled his view.

Jonah stumbled panting among the roots that rose like broken fingers above the black soil. Each breath was so heavy with the stench of excrement that he could hardly take it into his lungs. As he walked, the smell grew stronger, as did the hissing and the voice, which had now reached a screaming, incoherent pitch. He couldn't take it any longer. He clapped his hands over his ears, bent, and threw up.

He straightened up and went on. The voice had stopped, and now the trees thinned, revealing to him a clearing that was crowded with winged, horned creatures. At their center squatted an immense Baobab tree, and before it, wrapped in a cloak, stood the source of that unbearable voice—Lord Geist.

As Jonah stopped at the edge of the clearing, Geist raised one clawed hand. The Djinn fell silent and turned their heads to follow his gaze. Seeing Jonah, they began hissing again, their hostility rising until it filled Jonah's head and invaded his muscles, making them twitch.

"Well, Master Jonah," Geist said. At his voice, the Djinn's hissing died. "I came to you, and now you come to me. You took the long way around, but the end is the same." He held out one claw, from which now dangled the black pendant. "Are you ready to take me up on my offer?"

Jonah could barely get a reply from his closed throat.

"No," he croaked finally. "You took my father, and I have come to get him back."

Lord Geist shrieked with laughter, the Djinn host echoing him with a chorus of hisses. "You still don't understand how this works, do you?" he cried. "Or perhaps you don't *want* to understand...? If that is the case, then you should have taken the pendant to begin with... You chose the other way, and that means you *must* see things as they really are. Are you willing to do so?"

Jonah met Geist's empty eyes. "Yes. I am willing."

"Very good." Lord Geist nodded. "Deliberation is the fruit of maturity. Now deliberate upon what I have to say. In there—" he gestured to the Tree "—lies your father. He is asleep. In a moment he will have the nightmare that he has known every night since entering into our service. In that nightmare, you will see how I 'took' your father away from you and your mother. When you have considered the full implications of what you see, you may leave the tree, and we will continue our discussion about 'rescuing him.' Does that sound reasonable to you?"

Jonah stared at Geist. The Djinn host seemed frozen at the edge of his vision.

"What do you say, Master Jonah? Shall we be reasonable adults, thinking through our choices, or impulsive children?"

Jonah said nothing, but his legs carried him forward into the clearing, toward Geist and the Tree. Quickly, as if Jonah might change his mind at any second, Lord Geist dug into the tree and pulled the trunk open. Immediately, Francis's shouting and the stench inside hit them full force. Lord Geist gestured toward the black opening. Feeling faint and nauseous, Jonah stepped inside.

19

Chapter Nineteen

The light from outside briefly lit up a great mound of roots that filled the interior of the Tree. In their midst, entangled in them, his father's face was a pale, filthy blob, the rest of his body lost in the roots.

"Enjoy!" Lord Geist cried. Jonah turned to see the Elder Djinn pulling the Tree closed. Darkness came over them, then parted. Jonah found himself walking—or rather, he was looking through someone else's eyes as that person walked down a darkened hallway. He recognized the place at once as his own home. The person was taller than Jonah, but not until they passed the hallway mirror did Jonah realize that he was looking at the world through his father's eyes.

Francis Comfait reached Jonah's door and soundlessly turned the handle. Inside, Jonah's own form curled on the bed under a sheet. It was strange, almost dizzying to look at his own sleeping face. The light of dawn—pink and gold—spilled through the windows. His father looked for a moment—Jonah felt his heart beating and his fists clenching—then closed the door and moved on down the hallway, down the stairs, and out the front door to the old gray sedan in the driveway.

Francis started the car and began to back down the driveway. He gripped the steering wheel—slippery because he was sweating. Though he was starting to wish he could do so, Jonah could not control his father's movements. There was nothing to do but watch everything unfold through his eyes.

He knew what would happen next, but when the front door of the house swung open, and he saw himself running down the driveway, calling out, "Dad! Dad!" the certainty of it overwhelmed him.

His father put the brake on as Jonah ran up to the window.

"Why didn't you say goodbye, Dad? I was awake..."

"I checked," his father said. Jonah could hear the strain in his voice. "You were asleep. I didn't want to disturb you..."

"I don't care about that," Jonah cried. "You always say goodbye when you go!"

"I'm sorry," his father said. "The gentleman requested a quick fishing trip. We'll be back tonight. Promise."

"But what about the tropical storm they were talking about on the radio?"

"It'll be fine. We'll keep clear of its track. Alright?"

Jonah saw his own face frowning, suddenly sensing something amiss. "Is there something wrong, Dad?"

His father's voice was cheery but slightly brittle. "Don't be silly. I'm fine." From the way he continued to grip the wheel, though, Jonah knew he was lying. Francis must have doubted his own capacity to deceive because, at that moment, he forced one hand to let go of the steering wheel, reach out of the window, and ruffled Jonah's hair. "Now, I really have to go. Take care of your mother while I'm gone. Remember, you're the man of the house now."

"Yes, Dad," Jonah said, rolling his eyes and sounding resigned.

"I love you," his father said, and Jonah knew how much the words cost him.

"I love you too," Jonah replied automatically.

Then his father was backing the car away again, turning away from Jonah to watch where he was going. As he drove down the street, Francis glanced in the rear-view mirror, and Jonah saw his father's eyes were haunted. Then his father was looking back to where Jonah still stood, seeming lost and alone.

Francis drove along the sea road, the forest rising on his left up to the mountain and dropping on his right to the sea. He passed a few militia patrols who paid him no attention now that the curfew was over. The road rounded the headland and wound its way down to the city nestled in the bay.

Francis navigated the streets, driving quickly. They were still deserted apart from the occasional fisherman carrying his catch draped over a long pole to market. He turned right into the Marina, parked, and made his way down to the dock. No one was around this early, but Francis moved quickly. Jonah got the sense that he wanted to avoid unnecessary contact.

Integrity bobbed contently in her booth. As Francis went about readying the ship, Jonah relished the sensation of experiencing his father's quick and skillful movements as he tied ropes and hauled on the sheets. Within minutes, as the sun broke the horizon, he was standing at the wheel, backing *Integrity* out of her booth, the engine puttering quietly under her stern. He used power to guide the ship out of the Marina. When she was clear of the harbor buoys and heading to open sea, he killed the engine and hoisted the sails. They filled with the first breeze of the morning, and *Integrity* heeled, the water creaming against her lovely bow and burbling along her slender hull.

Jonah was so immersed in the experience of sailing his father's boat that he did not realize an obvious fact until a few hours into the journey, as they were passing the little isles that huddled closest to the main island. Then it struck him: *the tourist*. His father was alone on the ship...

He knew already that his father had lied, but the realization still left him cold. He tried to reason his way around, tried to find some kind of explanation, but nothing came to him. There had been no last-minute call for a fishing trip. As to why... Jonah didn't want to know the answer. He didn't want to see what happened next. He wanted to leave, but although he could feel himself turning away, reaching out, shouting for Geist to open the Tree—nothing came. He was forced to stand at the wheel of *Integrity*, looking through Francis's eyes over the ocean to the horizon, where purple thunderheads were clearly drifting across their course.

As the day progressed, the weather worsened. The sea turned a sullen green, exploding with ever greater intensity against the bows. The clouds scudded overhead, concealing the sun. The equatorial air was almost cold, a solid breath against his face. The inner islands disappeared below the horizon. They were navigating that empty stretch before the middle islands appeared.

Then, in the late afternoon, the storm itself hit in a screeching, shrieking blast of wind and water. It knocked *Integrity* onto her side and kept her there, heeled over, her leeward railing digging into the water. Despite this, his father did nothing to shorten the sail. He simply clung to the wheel as the storm-tossed and battered his ship, driving her before its implacable path. And finally, inexplicably, Francis closed his eyes, blotting out Jonah's ability to see anything.

What was he trying to do? Jonah thought. Francis's heart seemed to have come loose in his chest, every muscle strained. Jonah thought, *Was he going to...*

Then a familiar voice spoke. "Looking for a way out?"

Francis's eyes snapped open in terror, and Jonah saw Lord Geist in his human disguise, looking quite incongruous with his pale face and a full suit, but balancing easily on the steeply-tilted, storm-swept deck.

"Who are you?" Francis cried. "How did you get here?"

"I am a friend," Geist replied. "And I come and go quite easily. Would you like to come with me when I leave?"

"I'm not turning back!" Francis said. "This is the only way now!"

A massive breaker slammed the ship. The deck canted sharply. Francis slipped sideways, clinging to the wheel to stay upright. Geist never lost his balance or even moved, and Jonah realized his feet were not actually touching the deck. He was floating. He only *seemed* to be standing.

"The only way to what?" Geist asked.

"Liza thought I didn't know how bad it had gotten..." Francis seemed to be talking to himself. "But I knew it all along! I tried to make a go of it, but it wasn't enough. All I wanted was to keep the boat. Just the boat... But the hole kept getting deeper until I couldn't stand it anymore..."

"At the cost of your life?" Geist raised his eyebrows. "Sounds like a terrible bargain to me, my dear boy."

"I don't care!" Francis shouted. "After the insurance pays out, Liza and Jonah will never want for anything again!"

He was *going to kill himself*, Jonah thought. The horror of it filled every available space in his heart.

"I am not disputing your plan," Geist said, raising one placating hand, "merely your willingness to sacrifice your own life on top of everything else. Supposing you could have both?"

"Both?" Francis said. "What do you mean, both?"

Another breaker smashed against the ship. The deck was now almost vertical, Francis holding on for dear life.

Geist was still upright, his feet clearly floating above the air.

"What are you really?" Francis said. "A demon?"

"I am a Djinn," Geist said. "And I have an offer just for you. You see, I have been watching you, Francis Comfait. For many years, as a matter of fact, I have observed your thirst for something better. I mourned when you involved yourself with that old man and his Lamp, and I rejoiced when you gave up your misguided interest and returned to the main of life again. Then you became obsessed with finding Hodoul's treasure and I found myself wondering if you would ever amount to anything if you were worthy of my efforts. I was pleasantly surprised to see you establish your business, but it was obvious to me, if to no one else, what the real purpose of your endeavor was—to conceal your continuing addiction to that fantasy."

"There was real evidence—" Francis started.

"I was there when he was hanged," Geist said. "I know the man personally. He had *one* coin, and that was it! But I will not argue the point with you. The fact is, you never told your wife how obsessed you had become with finding a treasure that no one else could find. That foolish notion had stuck in your mind like a burr in a coat, itching you. For a while, you broke even, though you weren't even trying to drum up business. Then the dice turned against you, as they always do, but still, you went on digging. You invented bogus tours with phantom tourists so you could explore just one more island, one more possible lead to the fabled treasure... And what about the costs of those expeditions? You put them right out of your mind and left your wife to worry about it all, while you just went on digging yourself deeper and deeper until it was too late. You had buried yourself and your family alive..."

"I didn't mean to..." Francis said. Jonah could feel tears of self-pity coming to his eyes.

"Of course not!" Geist said. "No one ever does! But you did it nonetheless. And now, quite reasonably, you want a way out. That is where I come in. You see, I believe that you have accumulated a lifetime of debt looking for what I have to offer." He reached out his hand, from which now fell the chain, with its hungry, lightless stone dangling from the end.

"You have the treasure...?" Francis said.

"Take hold of this pendant," Geist said softly, "and I will take you to a world where you will find more treasure than you can imagine. In this world, your ship will be wrecked. The world will assume you are dead, and your wife and son will benefit from your untimely 'demise.' Meanwhile, you will be very much alive, living elsewhere, enjoying the riches you deserve."

"Where is this place?" Francis said, sounding desperate.

"Take the pendant, and you will see."

"What do you want in exchange?" Francis said.

"Just a little service..." Geist said vaguely. "At the end of which, you will be free to enjoy what you have earned."

"What kind of service?"

"Does it matter?" Geist said, sounding irritated. "Whatever I require."

"But—"

"I am out of patience, Francis. Take the pendant, or in three seconds, my offer will expire and I will disappear. One—"

"Wait!" Francis shouted. "Just tell me one more thing. In this place, this new life, will I remember what happened here?"

Geist spread his arms, grinning.

"That's the beauty of it. You will remember nothing. It will be as if you had woken from a nightmare and found yourself in a new life, making a fresh start, the comfort of your wife and child assured. Now for the last time, take the pendant. Two—"

With a sensation of watching his universe crumbling around him, Jonah watched his father's hand reach out.

"I'm sorry Liza, Jonah," Francis whispered. And he grabbed the stone.

Another wave, different from the others, tall and silent and all-encompassing, rose up out of the half-light and broke over the ship. Geist, *Integrity*, the fury and chaos of the storm, Jonah's vision—all vanished.

Jonah stood again in the Tree as Francis's cries echoed in the darkness.

20

Chapter Twenty

Jonah was overwhelmed by the smell—the acrid excrement of the hidden island combined with his father's odor of sweat and filth, of fear and despair. He fell on his knees and threw up until his throat was burning with bile. When there was nothing but spasms, he found himself unable to move.

There was a tearing sound. A gap of dusk appeared in the darkness as the trunk of the Tree was pulled apart. Beyond, Lord Geist stood, looking down at Jonah with satisfaction etched on his bony face.

"Now do you understand?" he said. Jonah said nothing, and he continued. "I did not *take* your father. I did not *trick* him. He took my offer to escape the hole he had dug, leaving you and your mother behind! If you want him back, you will have to pay for him..." Geist held out the pendant again. Jonah turned his head toward it. "Or else, you can go back to that old man with your tail between your legs and tell him you failed because your father turned out to be half the man you thought he was." He chuckled at his own joke. Behind, crowding close, the Djinn host broke into malicious laughter. Jonah was still on his knees.

"No child should see his father like this," Lord Geist said. "All children should remember their fathers well. If you take the pendant, I can help you to forget this." He gestured at the pile of roots behind Jonah, where Francis's head tossed back and forth as his nightmare consumed him. "More than that," Geist said, "I can help you to remember your father as he should be, as he once was perhaps...

"Give yourself to us, Jonah. Give yourself and I will give you a dream, unlike anything you have ever known. Your mother will adore you, your father will always be there to go sailing with you. You will inherit his ship and be successful in everything you do. You will have the love of a beautiful woman, adoring children. And you will die surrounded by your great-grandchildren."

Jonah finally found his voice. "But it wouldn't be true..."

"Who cares about truth when you can have happiness?" Lord Geist said.

"And what about my..." Jonah hesitated. "What about him?"

"He is almost used up. You know what that means, so you know he will very soon no longer be your father."

Jonah closed his eyes to block out the Djinn's face, but that bony, demonic head floated in his mind. He realized now that his horror was not shock. It was knowing that his worst fears had come true. Somewhere inside, since his first night on Captain Aquille's island, he had known why his father had gone with the Djinn. He had known that he had not been tricked.

His father had chosen to leave—that was the truth.

Suddenly, Jonah longed to forget. It would be easy for Geist to do. After all, what was left of the man he had called his father? And the more he chased the question, the further the answers receded.

Somehow the Elder had foreseen all this. So why, *why* had he sent Jonah here?

The Elder had said that whatever he lost, his love would open the prison. But was there anything left to love?

"I want to speak to him," Jonah said. "Before I do anything."

Geist's eyes narrowed. "Take my word for it. He has nothing to say."

"I don't care. I won't give anything until I'm sure you are right."

"Very well," Lord Geist said. "Talk to him." He snapped his fingers, and at once Francis's moans died away.

Jonah rose to his feet and went over to his father. He tried to say, "Dad," but the sound died in his throat.

Francis's eyes were open, staring unfocused. "Who are you?"

"I am Jonah." Then he made himself say it—"Your son."

"My son," Francis mumbled. "A good boy, that one."

"Dad." Jonah reached out and touched his father's shoulder. "I'm here."

"You came a long way, my son."

"Yes, I did."

"You learned to sail on the ocean. Well done!" Francis yawned.

Jonah felt the anger come over him. "I know what you did, Dad."

His father was silent. His eyes were still blank, looking but not seeing.

"I learned how to sail a long time ago," Francis said finally. "But I never got really good. Not like you."

"Dad..."

"I'm sorry, my boy. I am so sorry."

"That's not good enough." Jonah's voice shivered with anger and tears.

"I'm almost used up now, Jonah. Time for you to go home."

Jonah rose to his feet. "Yes," he said. He turned away from his father.

"Jonah."

Jonah stopped, but he did not turn back.

"Promise that you will ask your mother to forgive me one more time."

Suddenly, Jonah remembered something else the Elder had said. *Love is not really blind. It sees clearly and loves anyway.* Something gave way in his chest, and he knew at last what he had to do.

He turned back to look at his father. "I promise," he whispered.

"You learned to sail on the ocean," Francis murmured. "Just remember that. You learned how to sail by yourself."

"What is your answer?" Geist demanded.

Jonah turned to confront the Djinn.

"I won't take the pendant," he said.

"Very well then," Geist hissed. "You will leave now!"

"No," Jonah said. "I won't do that either."

Lord Geist gaped in disbelief. "What did you say?"

"I won't leave, and I won't take the pendant," Jonah said. "You let him go, and I will take his place."

Lord Geist looked uncertain for the first time. "Without a contract...? Are you insane, boy? That's insane..."

"You can either agree, or you can kill me," Jonah said. "Either way, I am not leaving without my father."

Geist looked back at the Djinn as if to confirm what he had heard. They were mute with confusion.

"What is *your* choice, Geist?" Jonah said.

Lord Geist caught a glimpse of Malach, smiling with amusement, and realized that his hesitation was costing him precious credibility. This seemed to galvanize him, and he rounded on Jonah.

"You're a fool, boy," he snarled. "But, if you want to throw yourself away for a liar and a coward, with no reward—"

He strode over to the mound of roots and began tearing them away. A moment later, he dragged Jonah's father free and tossed him onto the ground. As Francis struggled to rise, Jonah ran over to help him up.

"Jonah—" Francis said. "What did you do?"

"You're free, Dad," Jonah said softly. "I freed you."

"What do you mean?" his father said. "How—?"

"Your son is taking your place, free of charge," Lord Geist said. "How does it feel to have your own child pay your debt?"

Francis's eyes widened in horror. "No!" He turned to Jonah. "Jonah, I am still your father, and I forbid it!"

"Father?" Lord Geist scoffed. "You ran away from that responsibility, remember? Now, get up. You're leaving!"

As easily as one might lift a puppy by the scruff of its neck, Lord Geist jerked Francis, struggling and shouting, into the air. Just as effortlessly, he pulled Jonah off his father and tossed him into the roots. As soon as Jonah landed, the roots came alive, enveloping him, pushing into his skin. Jonah screamed. Lord Geist paused briefly at the opening of the

Tree to watch, while Francis dangled helplessly from his claw, sobbing and reaching out to Jonah.

Behind him, the Djinn were cheering.

"Enjoy your sleep," Lord Geist said. He pulled the Tree closed.

Jonah dropped into an abyss in the center of his mind, as if he were collapsing inwards. He moaned and reached out to stop himself, but his hands were gone. He was floating, disembodied, over a vast emptiness. Then a wind, like the beginning of the new monsoon, blew in his face, gathering strength. The darkness receded before the face of the wind, fading, fading...n, blew in his face, gathering strength. The darkness receded before the face of the wind, fading, fading . . .

21

Chapter Twenty-One

He was sailing his dinghy Albatross across a still ocean. His father was running beside him on the water, encouraging him, but Jonah could not understand his words. Then the boat capsized, and Jonah was in the water, drifting down through the sunbeams toward the ocean floor far below. Jonah looked up to see his father still standing on the ocean, looking down and smiling.

Jonah's chest ached from lack of breath. Then he coughed, and seawater flooded his nose and mouth. As his last breath bubbled from his lips, his struggle weakened. Then he knew he had died, and he was gliding like a seagull on outstretched wings. In death, he could see the ocean floor spread out beneath him like an endless moonlit wasteland, utterly empty.

A mermaid was swimming up toward him. It was Queen Zoë, with his mother's face. She finned gently up to him, took his head in both her hands, and kissed him on the lips. Then he was alive again, breathing slowly this time, water instead of air flowing between his lips.

His eyes spoke gratitude to the mermaid, who smiled in return and pointed down at the ocean floor. There was something standing on that dead plain. As Jonah floated down toward it, he saw that it was a tiny house with an onion-domed roof. But it was too small for a house...

It was the Lamp.

The mermaid's lips moved and her voice resounded in the dream. You lost this. I found it for you.

Jonah reached down and grasped the Lamp.

Thank you, he said in his dream.

The mermaid nodded. We will meet at your next death, new Elder.

Then he was rushing up toward the surface, carried on an endless breath of bubbles, the mermaid smiling up as he went.

He broke the surface. Now he was standing on the water. Around him, a great battled rage. On one side was an armada of metallic ships, bristling with cannons, the railings lined with armored warriors. On the other stood a ragged line of motley vessels—from schooners to fishing boats. The armada poured streams of fire onto the opposing vessels, most of which were already in flames. People leaped from the vessels, their bodies burning, to drown in the ocean. The screams of the wounded and the dying filled the air. Smoke billowed across the water and drifted over the sun, plunging the whole scene into a premature dusk.

Only then did Jonah look down. His parents were sitting at his feet, holding each other like frightened children and looking up at the sky. Jonah followed their desolate gazes and saw Lord Geist descending from the clouds on outspread wings, a drawn scimitar outstretched in his hand, leading the Djinn like a horde of locusts behind him.

Outside the Tree, the host of the Djinn cheered. The tree had started to change: small, spear-shaped leaves grew with remarkable speed from the main branches, sprouting bunches of black fruit.

Geist faced the Djinn host, watching them with satisfaction. Finally, he held up his hand for silence.

"Soon," Lord Geist said quietly, "we will feast."

The frenzied host hissed and danced up and down.

"But before then. We have a little justice to dispense..."

The Djinn snickered. They had dismissed Malach's plan to take control as too foolhardy against one as powerful as Lord Geist. Now they were ready to enjoy whatever punishment Lord Geist had planned.

"Malach. Bagat. Come forward!"

In the midst of the crowd, Bagat started and then froze. His head turned this way and that, looking for a way out, but his fellow Djinn pressed too closely, hemming him in. Beside him, Malach drew himself to his full height, staring coldly at Lord Geist. The others were parting now, but only to open a path that led directly to Lord Geist in front of the Tree.

"Please, my Lord..." Bagat shrieked. "I was deceived... It was him!" He pointed an accusing claw at Malach.

"Come on, you coward," Malach said, shoving him forward. "Come and take what's coming to you!"

"No!" Bagat shouted, but claws reached out from the crowd on either side, forcing him forward as Malach kicked at him from behind. The sounds of hissing and jeering rose to a crescendo of anticipation.

The Lamp floated before Jonah in the wind. He took it, thinking how weightless it was in a dream. And as if every movement had been predicted since the beginning, he lifted the Lamp toward the descending Djinn and started to blow. Instantly, the wick burst into flame.

Standing before Lord Geist, Malach refused to bow. Bagat, by contrast, pressed his face into the stinking black earth as if he hoped it would open up and allow him to burrow to safety.

"My Lord," he said, his voice muffled. "I had nothing to do with it... I told him... He's the real traitor!"

"And you?" Lord Geist said, turning to Malach. "Do you deny it?"

"No," Malach said. "I've wanted you dead for a long time."

The Djinn host gasped, then resumed their jeering, even louder than before.

"Very well," Lord Geist said. He pulled his cloak aside to reveal a gleaming scimitar. Peeping up from his prostration, Bagat saw the sword and uttered a loud shriek, squirming on the ground.

"Lord!" he screamed. "I beg you!"

"Here is what happens to those who disobey Lord Geist and betray their family!" And with what seemed like no effort, Geist beheaded Bagat in mid-scream. Bagat's severed head bounced sideways and crunched on the sand, blood spurting from his neck, even as his body tried to push itself up. Then Geist was on top of the body, slashing, tearing as blood splattered his face and cloak until Bagat was little more than a heap of shredded flesh and bones.

Jonah blew as if he contained a lifetime of breath within him. The flame in the Lamp's heart intensified swiftly, now blinding in its brilliance. And still the countless winged hosts of Djinn descended.

Lord Geist wiped the blood from his face with his cloak. He swept his gaze over the host, then turned to Malach, who stared straight ahead with defiance etched in every line of his skeletal face.

"I have kept the best until last," Geist whispered.

"Hurry," Malach whispered back. "Before your luck runs out!"

Geist grinned and raised the sword. "With this, our justice is complete!"

But as his stroke descended, one of the Djinn shrieked—"The Tree is burning!"

Lord Geist spun around.

As if igniting on some other substance, the Lamp erupted. Great spinning ropes of flame arced outward, whipping at the Djinn, who flapped backward, coming to a dead standstill. Then they retreated in terror, with Lord Geist in the rear, his face enraged as he looked back at Jonah.

The Tree's leaves and the fruit smoked, then burst into blue flame. Within seconds, the whole tree was consumed in a fire whose color and intensity Lord Geist remembered only too clearly. Many years before, he had seen a man—the one he had come to call the "tyrant"—holding up this Lamp for the first time, and this same fire had rolled toward Geist like a breaking wave. He remembered the agony of that defeat, the humiliation of exile, and felt a rockslide of disaster descending again as he watched the flame that he knew too well as Wind-Fire engulf his beloved Tree.

Inside the Tree, Jonah opened his eyes. The roots that had swaddled and penetrated his skin glowed, ignited, and then dissolved into ashes as he watched. He sat up, feeling refreshed, as if after a good night's sleep. Inside him, all the fear and pain had dissolved. A joyful serenity, an utter peace had taken over. He rose to his feet and stepped forward as the Tree smoked and burned around him.

Seeing the flames, the Djinn broke into a panic. They rushed forward, shoving and trampling on one another to snatch handfuls of black fruit from the burning branches, singeing themselves but seemingly inured to the pain. They gorged themselves, juice staining their mouths and running down their chins, then ran back for more. Within a minute, not a single fruit remained on the blazing branches.

Lord Geist and Malach held back from the fray. Lord Geist was mesmerized by the nightmare of watching his Tree consumed by Wind-Fire. Malach waited for the rush to die down, then sauntered over and picked up one of the pieces of black fruit that had fallen from the Tree and been trampled underfoot. Carefully, he examined the fruit, dug around inside it with a claw, and pulled out its seed. Then he tossed aside the meat of the fruit and pocketed the seed. He turned toward Lord Geist, but as he did so, the flames engulfing the Tree parted, and through them stepped a slight figure, taking calm measured steps.

The flames of Wind-Fire engulfed Jonah, burning through him. But there was no pain, just a vast serenity that enveloped and protected him. It was as if the Wind-Fire could not take hold of anything that might cause him pain.

Then the Tree was behind him. In front of him stood Lord Geist, rage and pain distorting his features.

"I don't know what trick you used for this, boy," the Djinn shrieked, "but you will never defeat *me*!" He flew toward Jonah with both claws extended toward Jonah's throat.

Malach landed on Geist like a giant pterodactyl. With a quick twist, he broke the Djinn Elder's neck. He hacked up Lord Geist on the ground before pulling the bloody cloak from the corpse and draping it around himself. Jonah braced himself, expecting Malach to continue the attack, but the Djinn only felt around in the cloak and pulled out the pendant that Lord Geist had offered to Jonah so long ago. Then he attempted to wink grotesquely.

"Well done, young man," he said. "You were the perfect distraction!"

He turned his back on Jonah and faced the host. Seeing Geist cut down had thrown them into a kind of madness. They milled aimlessly, hissing and shouting, jabbing fearful and accusing claws at Malach.

Then Malach raised his claw, and they instinctively fell silent before the authority of the cloak and pendant.

"My brothers!" he shouted. "We are free!"

The host shifted and muttered.

"From now on, we will answer to no one but ourselves! Free, brothers, and equal!" He paused to let his words sink in. "Our brother Bagat died at the hands of the tyrant Geist!" He gestured at the piles of bloody flesh and bones by his feet. He sensed that the mood was shifting, like the changing of the monsoon. Just a little push... "Do not let his sacrifice go in vain!"

Heads turned toward each other uncertainly.

Not quite enough, Malach thought. *Who cares about sacrifice?* As he furiously searched his mind for something to galvanize them, the solution arrived. The Wind–Fire had left the Tree a twisted, blackened hulk and now spread outwards like wings to consume the surrounding forest. It also rose upwards, burning off the clouds that cloaked the hidden island, and the morning sun showered down on Jonah and the Djinn. Pierced by the light, the Djinn whimpered and tried to hide. Only Jonah turned his face to the sky and smiled as the last of the island's darkness blew from his heart.

Something disturbed the steadiness of the sunlight, a flickering... Jonah squinted, held up his hand against the sun. Only then did he see that the sky was filled with brilliant, fluttering figures.

"Angeli," he whispered.

Malach, attempting to conceal himself from the light with his cloak, squinted upwards into the sky. He froze in horror, but only for a moment. He drew himself up and gestured upwards.

"Brothers!" he shouted. "You must now choose! You can stay and face the Angeli, who even now are upon us!"

The Djinn looked up and broke out into an ululation of terror.

"Or this!" Malach continued, holding up the seed he had picked up. The host stared at the seed with hungry desperation.

"We will find a new place," Malach cried. "We will replant this seed and continue our work. Who is with me!"

"We are with you, Lord!"

"Save us, Elder Brother!"

Malach pointed west, away from the Angeli. "Then we fly!"

He turned to Jonah. "We will meet again, Master Jonah. Perhaps you will remember my mercy to you." He and the Djinn rose into the air, collapsing into a swarm of bluebottles, wasps, and mosquitoes. They gathered around the seed and bore it away toward the west just as the Angeli descended to land. Azrel was in front, smiling at Jonah in that familiar sarcastic way of hers.

22

Chapter Twenty-Two

"Your father is safe," was the first thing Azrel had said, as she pulled him onto her back and rose out of the smoke of the hidden island. "I found him adrift in a boat outside the barrier of fire. He would have killed himself trying to get back through if we hadn't picked him up by force and taken him away. He's probably back at the Elder's Island already."

As they flew through the night, Jonah had recounted everything that had happened. Azrel had listened, for once offering few comments, but had occasionally glanced back with surprise and concern.

"The Djinn will be back," he said at last. "Malach said we would meet again."

Azrel nodded. "They will always come back. Until the Higher Mysterion comes."

"When?"

"No one knows. Not even the Elder."

"Perhaps never, then..."

"It will come!" Azrel insisted. "In time. Until then, we struggle on."

Jonah closed his eyes. He remembered the sensation of falling into the abyss inside himself when Geist had closed him in the Tree. That abyss would always be there, but so would the Wind.

"Are you all right?"

Jonah opened his eyes to see Azrel looking back at him in concern.

"I feel old," he said, smiling lopsidedly. "Older than my own father."

Azrel nodded. "Because you live in Mysterion now. And Mysterion is older than all time that you have known."

"What?" Jonah frowned.

"Never mind. Rest now."

Suddenly, exhaustion collapsed on him like a landslide. His head sank onto Azrel's fluttering shoulders.

"Azrel?" he murmured, after a moment.

"Yes?"

"I like you," he said.

He could hear the grin in Azrel's voice. "You're not so bad yourself, shrimpy."

"And then you have to go and say things like that..." he murmured.

Jonah woke to the softness of a bed. He was lying in the bower where he had slept the first night in Mysterion. Beyond the open doorway, the Seeing Pools glinted among the trees in the distance.

A hand gripped his shoulder. His father squatted beside him, his face pale and haggard, his eyes underlined by lack of sleep—the way Jonah's mother had looked for days after he left.

His father held out a bowl overflowing with fruit. "Breakfast," he said.

Still groggy, Jonah pushed himself up and took a piece of fruit. It was delicious—bright-tasting—and by the time he was finished, Jonah was sitting straight, his eyes on his father, ready for what came next.

"I didn't want that to happen to you, Jonah," Francis said.

"I know," Jonah said. "But I wanted it."

His father looked down. "I don't know why you would."

"You are my father," Jonah replied simply. "And you taught me to sail, remember? Speaking of which, I crossed the reef at home in

Albatross. She's not bad on the open water, you know."

"Really?" The trace of a smile lit Francis's face.

"I sailed her all the way to Captain Aquille's island."

"Tell me," his father invited.

🔥 🔥 🔥

Later, they walked together to the gazebo. Azrel flew slow circles above, along with several other Angeli.

She waved at Jonah as he approached. "Finally awake, eh? You're definitely one of those teenagers, aren't you?"

"I work for a living," Jonah replied, grinning. "You should try it some time."

Azrel laughed and circled in delight.

As he approached the doorway, Jonah saw someone he recognized and ran forward to grip his hand.

"Sartish!" he said. "You made it!"

Sartish grinned and rocked his head. "I was finding my way. With a little help."

"The mermaids?" Jonah guessed.

"Yes," Sartish said. "They brought me on the strangest journey. I think I may have died at some point..."

Jonah remembered his dream in the Tree and nodded. "It wouldn't surprise me."

Sartish shook his head. "I would never have believed it."

Jonah laughed. "Me neither. And this is just the beginning..." Then his eyes fell on the Elder, lying on his couch. The old man looked frailer than ever, so pale as to be almost translucent...

Sartish saw the direction of his eyes and nodded in understanding. "You go and see him. Time to talk later."

Jonah nodded. "Thanks, Sartish." He gripped his friend's shoulder one more time and went in to kneel at the old man's couch. Sartish and Francis hung back just outside the doorway.

"So, my boy," the Elder said. "You did it."

"Yes, Sire," Jonah said.

"You did well. I never doubted it."

"Did you know, Sire?" Jonah said.

"Know what?"

"What would happen, from the very beginning."

The Elder smiled. "Not in a Seeing Pool kind of way, if that's what you mean. But I am a pretty good judge of character, Jonah, and you have a good character. You listen to the Wind."

Jonah shook his head. "I don't understand that."

"It means that you are willing to see things as they really are. In your father..." he glanced over at Francis, who lowered his head slightly, "...but more importantly, in yourself. That is how you defeated the Djinn."

Jonah frowned. "But you said that without the Lamp, *I* would be defeated."

"And you were defeated," the Elder said. "Or rather, you accepted defeat. But not all defeats end in destruction. Yours was a defeat in the name of love, and those kinds of defeats always end in victory."

"But how?" Jonah said.

"You gave yourself to the Djinn, but only those who *sell* themselves are imprisoned." Jonah saw his father wince as the old man said these words. "Geist thought he was getting a free slave, but what he failed to understand was that there is no such thing. A slave is *always* paid for. That is why his tree failed to imprison you. It was like pouring seawater on a healthy plant. The Tree needed to feed on your slavery to thrive. You fed it on love and destroyed it."

Jonah looked at his father, who had been listening to the conversation with his eyes fixed on the ground. Francis Comfait seemed to feel his gaze, looked up and pursed his lips, then lowered his eyes again.

"I had a dream," Jonah said. "The Lamp was at the bottom of the ocean, and Queen Zoë gave it to me..."

"Not so strange," the Elder said, and he gestured at something beside the couch, draped with a red cloth.

Jonah lifted away the cloth. "The Lamp!"

"The Blind Watchman did not remember what it was," the Elder said. "Memory is not a strong suit with his race. However, the mermaids found it and returned it to us, along with your friend over there... Besides, this Lamp can never really be lost. Even when it is buried or sunk in the depths of the sea, we can still find it in our dreams, as you discovered. And now it is yours."

"But..." Jonah hesitated. "The Tree is destroyed. The Djinn are defeated."

"Sadly, no," the Elder sighed and shook his head. "The Djinn will find a new island and grow a new Tree and continue to use it to harvest the Lethes. Which is why there is still work to be done."

"What work?" Jonah said.

"*My* work," the Elder said. "It is yours now. I am tired, and it is time for me to rest and return to the Wind."

Jonah shook his head. "But I don't know the first thing..."

The Elder waved. "Of course you do. There's still some growing up to be done, certainly, but once that happens, you will be perfectly capable. I have no doubt you will know exactly what to do."

"I can't..." Jonah said, desperation in his voice.

"Yes, you can," the Elder said firmly. "You will take the Lamp, and tonight, you will enter Sleep and return to the world of the Lethes. You will live there until you next kindle the Lamp. Then you will wake in Mysterion again, where only one night will have passed here, and it will be morning. And here you will rule as the New Elder in my place, until the Higher Mysterion."

Jonah closed his eyes. "I'm just not ready..."

"Of course not," the Elder said, waving. "But the Wind will complete what is lacking in you. Now," he said, becoming suddenly brusque and stern. "My time is over. Yours is now. Take the Lamp."

Jonah stared at him for a long moment, then reached out, his heart racing, and picked up the Lamp.

"Good!" the Elder said. "Now, let's introduce the New Elder to his people. Lend me your shoulder, will you?"

With great effort, the Elder sat up, then rose to his feet, putting his weight on Jonah. They made their way to the door and down the steps. Sartish and Francis followed them, walking a pace behind as they made their way over the plateau to where it dropped away into the cliff.

Azrel and the Angeli continued to hover and circle above.

"Sire," Jonah said in a low voice, as they walked. "What about my father? What will happen to him?"

The old man glanced over his shoulder at Francis, who met his eyes, then looked away, his face pale.

"He has a choice," the Elder said. "He can go west, or east. Going west will take him to the pirates, where he was destined to go. Going east... That's a little harder. A *lot* harder, actually."

"What's east?" Jonah said.

"Himself, and his redemption," the Elder said. "He knows all this. We have spoken about it."

Jonah looked back at his father, who nodded, his eyes sad but resolved.

They reached the edge of the plateau. Far below, at the base of the cliff, a crowd had gathered. Men and women of all ages and varieties, children darting around among them, all with their faces turned up toward them. When the Elder raised his hand in greeting, they sent out a great cheer.

"Long live Jonah!" they shouted. "Long live the Elder!"

At last, their cheers subsided and the Elder spoke. "My children," he said. "As you know, I must leave you today." He did not raise his voice, yet it seemed to resound inside Jonah's head. The crowd must have heard him the same way because now even the children were still.

"But today I give you a new Elder." The Elder pointed to Jonah. "You have heard his name, and you have learned how he defeated the Djinn." The Elder grasped Jonah's hand with the Lamp and raised it.

"He is worthy!" he shouted.

"He is worthy!" the people roared in reply.

As if the words were a signal, a wind rose up, encircling Jonah and the Elder. As it picked up speed, accelerating into a whirlwind, the crowd raised its voice again, but this time with grief, many of them waving and weeping at the same time as their voices cried out, "Long live the Elder!"

Still, the whirlwind grew in intensity. Jonah could no longer see his father or Sartish outside of it. Only above could he still see the Angeli circling, giving him the distinct impression that they had caused the whirlwind. Beside him, the Elder's form had blurred, as if the wind were smearing him somehow. Then he dissolved into streams of color, blown away in the wind. For a moment, the old man's smile remained before he vanished. A faint echo of his voice resounded in the air as if the wind itself were speaking:

In the Higher Mysterion...

The whirlwind rose upward, followed by the Angeli. Azrel was the last to ascend, smiling her farewell as her mouth formed the words that spoke directly into Jonah's mind: *You are worthy after all.*

And then the whirlwind and the Angeli rose out of sight, vanishing into the brilliance of the morning sun.

23

Chapter Twenty-Three

L ater that afternoon, Jonah stood on a deserted beach on the eastern side of the island, watching his father make final preparations to sail. The boat was a small fishing vessel with a single sail, and it bobbed half in and out of the surf, its prow pointing at the ocean as if eager to set sail.

The sun floated down to the horizon in a blaze of old gold, turning red at the edges. Jonah had tried to convince his father to wait until morning, but Francis had been resolute. He had to go as soon as possible, and he had already decided to go east, wherever it might take him.

Francis finished tying off the sheets and checking his stores of fruit and coconut before turning to Jonah. They regarded each other in silence, for once awkward in each other's presence, keeping a distance between them. The moment was too heavy for any words. Both of them knew that the departure had to be, and why it had to be. And still, the sadness blocked out everything else.

"How long?" Jonah said at last, though he knew the answer to that as well.

Francis shrugged and shook his head. "As long as it takes. I took the Djinn's way here. I have to find my own way back. No excuses this time. No running away. Whatever I have to do, I will do it..."

Jonah ran forward and hugged his father.

"I will be waiting for you," he whispered.

At first surprised, his father returned the hug with equal fierceness and something that felt like gratitude.

"Thank you, son," he said, his voice trembling with emotion. "But if your mother wants to... move on..."

"I'll tell her what happened," Jonah said quickly. "She'll understand."

"Still, Jonah," his father said, pulling away so that he could meet Jonah's eyes. "Don't hate her if she doesn't."

Jonah looked at him.

"Okay," he said finally. "But I still don't like Harry."

His father smiled with one corner of his mouth. "You don't have to. But at least try to get along with him. He's not so bad, really..." As if the thought had reminded him of something he should be doing, a resolute expression came over Francis's face. He pulled away. "I should be going before the sun sets."

Jonah dropped his arms to let him go. Francis bent and kissed the top of Jonah's head. "I love you, my son."

"I love you too, Dad."

Francis shoved the boat into the water and leaped aboard. He sculled the tiller to steer her away from the wind. The sail filled with a quiet *snap* and she was off, water creaming on her bow. Once he was settled on course, Francis turned one last time and raised his hand in farewell.

Jonah waved back. He watched his father sail away until he was nothing but a speck, soon swallowed by the sunset.

That night, as Jonah watched the people feasting and laughing at the long tables piled with an abundance of fish and fruit and wine, he felt a strange duality. There was a lightness in seeing them so carefree. Despite their grief at the Elder's departure, they seemed to trust that he was not really gone. And they had quickly transferred their childlike trust in the old man to Jonah. Already, more than one of them had come to him for counsel on a few small matters, confident that he could answer them as well as the Elder had before him. Jonah had felt completely unqualified to answer any of them and had said so, but this had done nothing to disillusion them—they knew that he would answer when ready. "Listen to the Wind," they had said, "and then tell us what it says."

So he watched them now with a genuine pleasure, a deep sense that they were *his* people to grow with and love until the Higher Mysterion. At the same time, there was a weight, a darkness, and he knew he could not share in their joy. His experiences over the past days had shown him too much of the darkness that still lurked beyond the light of the lanterns hung on ropes over the tables and the dancing space, where now the groups of men and women were lining up opposite each other, and the fiddler was tuning his instrument. Somewhere out there, he knew, was a humming swarm of evil looking for a place to come to earth. And, in whatever place they landed, they would spread their filth and smoke and fire, and the Tree would grow again...

One day the Djinn would break the curse that kept them in exile and return to cover this joy in darkness. Knowing all this, Jonah watched the dancers moving in time to the fiddler's tune, smiling and clapping with the others, even as he was aware of what would be coming to sweep it all away. He knew it would always be this way, and he would have to live with it—until the Higher Mysterion.

Beside him, Sartish must have understood, because he reached out and rested a hand on his shoulder. Jonah turned to him and saw that his friend's smile was tinged with the same sadness.

"You have work to do," he said. "Let me do the worrying for you."

Jonah nodded and returned the smile. Once the dance was in full swing and the audience had gathered close to encourage the dancers with rhythmic claps, he rose and slipped away into the darkness, heading in the direction of the bower.

He did not see the little girl, Shantih, slip away to follow him. When she arrived at the bower, Jonah was already asleep. Softly, she went over and settled herself beside him.

"I will care for you," she murmured, searching his face with eyes that seemed far older than her age. "As I did for him."

Jonah sighed, but his eyes remained closed.

"Sleep well, Sire," she said and blew into his face.

24

Chapter Twenty-Four

At daybreak, Jonah's mother Elizabeth looked out to sea, as if she could hear something just beyond the horizon.

She heard a crackling and turned. A balding, pear-shaped man was approaching over the fallen coconut fronds. He wore white linen pants and a white short-sleeved shirt, his peaked cap tucked under his arm.

The captain of the Coast Guard pulled out a handkerchief and mopped the rivers of sweat running down his forehead. He tucked the handkerchief away and wiped a hand back over his hair to smooth it.

They stood in silence for several minutes.

"The Bishop sends his regards," he said at last.

"You met him?" Elizabeth asked without turning her eyes from the horizon.

"He was blessing a boat at the dock."

"Oh." She glanced sideways. "That's all he said?"

The Coast Guard Captain hesitated. "He also said that he's willing to hold a memorial for your son whenever—"

Elizabeth Comfait shook her head. "Not yet."

The Coast Guard Captain was silent. "It's been three weeks."

"I know how long it's been."

"And you know that I will search as long as is necessary."

"It's all right, Captain Joubert."

She turned, and he was disturbed by the calm in her eyes.

"You mean... call it off?"

"No."

"I don't understand."

She pointed across the water at Isle Decouvre. "Did you search there?"

"Of course," Captain Joubert replied. "No sign of Jonah's boat and the old man wasn't at home."

"Try again," she said.

"Madame..."

"This time, I will come with you," she said. There was no trace of weeping in her heart-shaped face. The morning sun rising from the sea lit up her features, perfectly serene. "And we will find him."

"How do you know?" he asked.

Elizabeth turned her eyes back to the water.

"Because someone sent me a dream."

25

Chapter Twenty-Five

Shantih's breath swept down into Jonah's unconsciousness and woke him into an active state of dreaming. Now he was falling through a primordial darkness as Shantih's breath whirled around him.

The darkness parted, and he was falling through daylight. Below, the ocean was a limitless blue. Closer, an island appeared in the blue, the panorama swelling and expanding. Now he was rushing down toward the shore—a tiny strip of sand. Two people lay side by side, one slumped over. Between them was a brilliant object like a miniature fallen sun. The Lamp.

He recognized Captain Aquille, and then the other person—himself—the moment before he fell into himself and...

He opened his eyes.

Nearby, the Lamp gleamed, though no longer with the world-transforming light he had seen before. Only sunlight played over its surface now. On the sand beside him, Captain Aquille looked as if he had fallen asleep, still seated but bent forward and leaning slightly to one side.

Jonah took a deep breath and exhaled. Gently, he leaned forward and touched one of the old man's hands.

"We will meet in the Higher Mysterion," he murmured.

26

Chapter Twenty-Six

As the sun descended toward the horizon in a blaze of colors, the Coast Guard rounded the headland and entered the little bay. It sounded its horn. On the beach, Jonah held the body of Captain Aquille against himself and watched it come. Then he noticed his mother standing at the bow, and he smiled and waved.

The ship dropped anchor and the crew scrambled to launch the rescue dinghy. Within minutes the dinghy was racing in to shore, and within an hour after that, they were motoring back to the ship with Jonah sitting amidships beside the old man's body, now sealed in a canvas body bag. His mother watched him come. As they approached, he saw that her cheeks were wet with tears.

Captain Joubert helped him on board, looking bewildered.

"I don't understand," he said. "Have you been here the whole time, young man?"

Jonah nodded wearily.

"But... we searched the whole island. You were nowhere to be found!"

"Perhaps the Wind hid us from your sight," Jonah said.

The confusion deepened in the man's face. He began to say something, but Jonah was already turning to go his mother. She wore one of her white dresses with red roses. The black dress was gone. As he came up to her, she pulled him close and held him in silence. Finally, he drew away and searched into her green eyes, wondering at her serenity, but saw nothing in them but joy and tears.

"Aren't you supposed to be angry at me?" he said, frowning.

"Why should I?" she replied. "I knew where you were."

Jonah frowned wonderingly. "How did you know?"

"I had a dream," she said. "A very strange dream about a world even more beautiful than this one. I saw creatures too strange to describe, and I saw an old man—his face was too bright to see completely, but I knew him. He told me things I could not understand, but when I woke up, somehow..." she hesitated, "I knew what he meant, even though I could not explain. Dreams can be like that sometimes," she shook her head, "but this was different. In spite of everything, all the bad news, I knew that when the time came, I would be able to find you again."

So she did know, in her own way, Jonah thought. *Maybe one day I can tell her the rest.* And he hugged her close again.

As the ship made full speed away from Isle Decouvre, Jonah and his mother stood in the bow, her arm about his shoulders. Occasionally, she glanced down at him, as if to confirm that he was really there. Jonah, feeling her gaze, turned to meet her eyes and smiled. Beside him on the deck stood his new companion, the Lamp, its surface reflecting golden red in the light of day.

His mother glanced down at the Lamp. "Where did you get that?"

"It was a gift from the Captain," Jonah said. "I used it to find Dad."

"And where was he?" she said, staring ahead at the horizon.

"He was in Mysterion," Jonah said.

"Mysterion..." she repeated and smiled. "Sounds like something from a dream."

"In a way, it is," Jonah said. "A dream about the world as it really is."

Elizabeth nodded. She seemed to understand.

"And," she said, "I take it he didn't want to come back?"

As Jonah considered how to answer, he imagined his father setting out toward the east in his fishing boat, the setting sun shining on his face. Had Francis summoned the courage to find what the Elder had promised? Or had fear led him to turn his boat around and sail west to join the pirates, as he had been destined to do? Although he could not answer for certain, Jonah felt hope.

"Yes," he said finally. "He did. But he had to find something first. Then he said he would come home."

"Well," his mother said. "Let's hope he finds what he's looking for."

"He'll find it," Jonah said. "At the end of his journey."

27

Chapter Twenty-Seven

Days later, Jonah walked down to the beach, carrying his Lamp. The sun had set behind the mountains. The water was calm all the way out to the reef. Jonah made his way along the sand to a large Takamaka tree.

At the base of the tree, he rolled aside a round granite boulder, exposing a hollow, and pulled out a catapult, bow and arrows, a model sailboat, a tangle of fishing line, a hook, and a bait tin. Into the space, he slipped the Lamp and concealed the hollow again. He gathered up his old toys and walked back toward the head of the beach, his feet sinking in the sand above the high tide mark.

Before turning onto the sea road, he paused and looked back to the shadow of Captain Aquille's island on the horizon. Then he walked home. When he arrived, the lights were on. In the upstairs window, his mother moved back and forth. Jonah tried to catch her eye with a wave, but Elizabeth did not see him in the dark. She disappeared from view, but she soon reappeared downstairs as she went through into the kitchen to finish making supper with Madame Paul.

He stopped at the front door and listened. Shadows filled the garden. In the mango trees, crickets chirruped. Doves cooed among the coconut fronds, and somewhere in that cacophony, he heard a sound—the wind blowing like a hurricane somewhere far above him in Mysterion.

Jonah listened for a long time. Clutching his childhood toys closer, he smiled and sighed—a single, long breath.

"Mysterion is real," he whispered. And he stepped into the house.

Get a Free Gift!

Sign up for my exclusive Reader's Group, and I'll send you an audio excerpt of the next book in the series, FOR FREE. *The Falls of Mysterion* continues the journey started in the first book, and available only to my subscribers.

As a part of my Reader's group, you'll get exclusive access to advanced copies of future books in the series, and you'll be able to contribute to my creative process, including world-building and character design. Plus, you'll be first in line to get all kinds of free swag that I'll give out on a regular basis.

To get your free gift, join the Reader's Group now at **http://eep-url.com/cTN5X1**

Did you enjoy this book? You can make a big difference!

Reviews are the most powerful tools that I have when it comes to getting attention to my books. Although I'm not a starving artist, I don't have the financial muscle to take out full page ads in the *New York Times*.

But I do have something more powerful than that.

A committed, excited, and loyal group of readers.

Honest reviews of my book help bring it to the attention of new readers. The more reviews it has, the more Amazon "notices" it. At a certain point of interest, the Amazon algorithm can actually help make my books "more discoverable."

If you've enjoyed my novel, I invite you join my Reader Group by signing up here: **http://eepurl.com/cTN5X1**

I would also be very grateful if you'd spend only five minutes to leave a short review on the book's Amazon and Goodreads page. You can jump straight to that page by clicking below:

amazon.com/author/www.richardgarciamorgan.com

https://www.goodreads.com/rgarciamorgan

Thank you very much!

Made in the USA
Monee, IL
27 August 2021